Merry
HEARTS

AMBER KELLY

Visit my website at www.authoramberkelly.com
Cover Designer: Sommer Stein
Cover Image: Michaela Mangum, Michaela Mangum Photography
Editor: Jovana Shirley, Unforeseen Editing, www.unforeseenediting.com
Proofreader: Judy Zweifel, Judy's Proofreading
Formatter: Champagne Book Design

To Autumn Gantz, an amazing publicist and a kick-ass friend. I don't know what I'd do without you.

Merry
HEARTS

One

SOPHIE

I REACH INTO THE BOX, PULL OUT ANOTHER TANGLED STRING OF lights, and huff.

"Were Braxton and Walker drunk when they took the tree down last year?" I yell.

"Probably," Elle answers as she comes down the hall with Lily Claire in her arms.

Hawkeye trails behind them, right on Elle's heels.

"Straightening out this mess is going to take forever," I grumble as I work at removing the worst knot.

"I don't know how you get anything done. All I'd want to do is hold her every second of the day," she says as she cuddles her niece.

"Rocking her and feeding her are pretty much all I do get done nowadays. That's why the house is a wreck, and I look like one of the characters on *The Walking Dead*," I reply.

"You do not. Other than the dried spit-up in your hair and the pizza stain on your pajama pants, you look amazing."

I laugh. "Thanks."

She sits on the sofa, and Hawk jumps up beside them and lays his head on her leg. He is never far from the baby. Wherever she goes, he goes. He has even taken to sleeping on the floor beside her bed instead of with Braxton and me. Which shocked us both, but he's been protective of her since she was in my tummy. He battled a rattlesnake to keep it from striking while I was pregnant and lost the sight in his right eye as well as the hearing in his right ear.

Once I get the lights untangled, I walk over to the closest receptacle and plug in the strand, seeing that it illuminates immediately. I set it in the Working pile before I return to sit in front of the boxes of holiday decor.

A hiccup escapes Lily Claire before a loud burp, and Elle starts to giggle.

"You sound like your daddy," she coos at the baby.

Lily Claire smiles.

"Yeah, she looks and acts like him too. She has the same grin and the same hot temper. I carried her for nine and a half months and pushed for six straight hours, but she decides to be his spitting image. Rude."

"I think she has the Lancaster nose, and her hair is probably going to be light, like yours," Elle says.

"You can't possibly tell that."

"Both Braxton and I were born with a head full of dark hair." She shrugs.

I stop to consider that for a moment as I turn to look at my daughter's perfectly bald head. I smile to myself because I like the thought of her having at least one feature that comes from me. I, too, was bald until the age of two, and in every picture of me from two to five years old, my mother put a bow into my fine white-blonde hair, making the tiny bit stick straight up. I looked like my head had sprung a leak.

"Well, hopefully, her temper will calm down, and she'll have my disposition too. I don't think I can live with two stubborn Youngs," I tease as I fish ornaments out and separate them by color.

"What was that?" Braxton's voice comes booming in as the

front door launches open, and he leads the top of the tree into the living room with Walker bringing up the rear.

"What?" I ask as I jump to my feet.

He guides the tree to the bay windows that look out over our backyard, and he and Walker stand it up to its full height. They did it. They found a gorgeous, full blue spruce that reaches almost to the top of our two-story living space.

Walker secures the tree to the base as Braxton holds it in place.

"Don't play innocent with me. I heard you call me stubborn," Braxton says before he lets go of the tree and pulls me into him.

I shrug before I kiss his jaw.

"Do you like it?" he asks.

"I love it; it's perfect for Lily Claire's first Christmas tree," I say as I look up at the branches.

"I think so too," he says proudly.

Walker stands back and admires their work.

"Took all morning with this ass critiquing every damn tree on the side of the mountain. That one's too short; that one's too skinny; that one is shaped funny. You'd have thought he was picking a wife, not a tree."

"You were just as bad as I was," Braxton accuses.

Walker just shrugs. "Well, that's one down and three to go. We'd better get back to it," he states.

"Three?" I ask.

"Yes, ma'am. We still have to get one to Doreen and Ria, my mom, and my place for Elle and me."

"Sounds like you guys have a full day ahead of you." I grimace.

Braxton works the family ranch, Rustic Peak, sun up to sun down all week, and Sunday is his only day to spend with Lily Claire and me.

He runs his fingers up my neck and lifts my chin. "I promise I'll hurry, so I can get home, and we can decorate the tree tonight."

Uh-oh, I guess it's time to come clean. I've been dreading this, but here goes nothing.

"I told Mom we'd wait for her and Stanhope before we trimmed the tree," I break to him gently.

He frowns.

I knew he wasn't going to be happy with that news.

"I thought we settled this already?" he asks as he lets me go and takes a step back.

"I know it's our first Christmas with the baby, and you wanted to start all of our traditions, but this is the first year in forever that they want to spend Christmas at home instead of on a tropical beach, and I want it to be a family Christmas. Mom pleaded with me to let them do the tree with us, and you know I have a hard time telling her no."

"Well, I don't. Get Viv on the phone," he demands.

Crap. I walked right into that one.

"I can't. She and Stanhope are already on a plane. They'll be here in a few hours," I whisper as I try to hold back tears. It doesn't take much to cause the waterworks lately.

"They're already on a plane?" he bites out.

"I think that's my cue to go wait in the truck. You want to come and give me some good-bye sugar, woman?" Walker asks Elle as he walks around us to the front door.

"Yep, we'll see you off," Elle agrees as she stands with the baby, and she and Hawk follow him.

I watch them exit and shut the door before I look back to Braxton's fiery eyes.

"How are they already en route to Poplar Falls before you even bothered to tell me they were coming?" he asks.

"It's my mother. She didn't call to tell me they were on their way until they were on the runway, about to take off," I start to explain.

"We settled this over a week ago, Sophie. Did you not tell her we wanted to spend our first Christmas alone?"

"I tried. But she pointed out that Daddy and Madeline and the rest of our family will get to spend it with us. Which is true, and to be fair, I think they should get to come if they are willing."

"That's different, and you know it. The rest of the family have their own homes and aren't in our space. Where do they plan to stay?"

"Here, of course," I answer.

"Here? Not a hotel?"

"I'm not asking them to stay at a hotel when we have three extra bedrooms, Braxton. That's just ridiculous. They never make me get a hotel room when I'm in the city. They make me feel completely welcome at their home."

"They can stay at the ranch, then. There is plenty of room over there," he suggests.

"You can't be serious. You want my mother to stay in Daddy and Madeline's house?"

"They won't care."

"Oh my God, yes, they will. And even if they said it was okay, my mother would flip her shit. Stop being an ass, Mr. Grinch."

"I'm not the one being unreasonable. It's my daughter's first Christmas. It's our first holiday as a family. I want to start our traditions, just the three of us."

"Braxton, it's my mom. She's Lily Claire's grandmother, and she hasn't even seen her granddaughter—who was named after her—in person yet. And you're right. It's her first Christmas. I want all the people who love her to be here for it while they are healthy and alive and can be," I explain as my tears finally give up the fight and roll down my cheeks.

He sighs loudly. "Fine. We'll wait for them," he says as he stomps past me.

"Braxton!"

He turns, and I can see the anger rippling off of him like waves.

"Please don't be mad," I plead.

He doesn't respond; he just grabs the handle and walks out, slamming the door behind him.

I flinch and stare after him until the door opens slowly, and Elle emerges.

"Looks like that went over well," she says.

"As well as I thought it would." I sniffle.

"I'm sorry my brother is such a jackass sometimes. You want me to have a stern sister-to-brother talk with him? Or better yet, I can tattle to Aunt Doreen and Aunt Ria and let them deal with him," she asks.

That makes me laugh. "Thanks for the offer, but he's my husband, and I can handle him myself. I think these postpartum hormones have thrown me off my game. I'll pull myself together before he gets home tonight, and I'll set him straight. Don't worry," I tell her.

"That's my girl," she says as she bounces Lily Claire. She whispers to her, "Us women have to stick together and show them boys who's boss."

The phone rings, and I walk to the kitchen to get it.

"Hello?"

"Hi, little momma." Charlotte's chipper voice comes over the line.

"Hey, Char," I greet my business partner and one of my best friends.

"How's my goddaughter today?"

"Perfect. She's currently curled up in her aunt Elle's arms, taking a power nap."

"God, I wish I were there. I hate that it's going to be another month before I get to meet her. Dallas is going to have her all convinced that she's her favorite before I have a chance to spoil her rotten."

"Dallas has her hands full with her own baby right now. I think you're safe," I assure her.

My best friend, Dallas Wilson, gave birth to her daughter, Faith, a couple of months before Lily Claire came along.

"It's fine. I can totally compete. I'll just pull out the big guns once she's a little older."

I don't dare guess what Charlotte considers the big guns.

"Anyway, I was calling to tell you that I set up a meeting with the new marketing firm on Wednesday before we close up shop for the holidays. I'll video conference you in, so be sure to brush your hair and put on some real clothes."

"Ugh, I guess I can do that, but call me an hour before and make sure I'm not napping. Lily Claire has her days and nights mixed up, and she wants to party like a rock star all night long and sleep her milk hangovers off all day."

She laughs. "She is totally going to love me best. She's already my spirit animal."

"I'll FaceTime you tonight, so you can see her when we light the tree for the first time," I offer.

"Yes, please do. I miss you guys. I wish you weren't a three-hour plane ride away," she whines.

"Me too, but you'll be here in February, and that's not that far away."

"Okay, I'm at spin class, so I'm going to let you go. Squeeze that baby for me, and I'll call you on Wednesday."

"Sounds good."

I hang up the phone and smile to myself. I have a secret surprise for Charlotte that she isn't expecting. It will be arriving Wednesday night, and I can't wait for her to find out what it is. She's going to freak out.

I join Elle back in the living room.

"I'm going to lay her in her crib and come help you. What do we need to conquer first?" she asks.

I look around. "I have to get these decorations sorted, this house semi-clean, and myself bathed before Mom and Stanhope arrive."

"How long do we have?"

"They land in Denver in three hours," I tell her.

"Great! Then, there's the drive out to Poplar Falls, so that gives us about five hours. Plenty of time to get everything ready."

"Thank you, Elle. I appreciate you spending your Sunday with us."

"There's nowhere else I'd rather be."

Two

WALKER AND I RIDE IN SILENCE TO THE RANCH. He pulls up in front of the main house and parks just as Doreen, Ria, and Pop step out on the porch.

"Oh, we were hoping you guys would make it here soon," Ria says as she descends the steps to the driveway.

Walker and I exit the truck cab and walk around and meet her at the back, where three trees remain.

"These are gorgeous. You two did so well," she squees.

"Which one do you want?" Walker asks.

"Hmm, let me see. This one looks nice and full. Oh, but that one is taller. Goodness, Doreen, you come and decide," Ria calls as she fusses over the choices.

Doreen joins us and assesses them. "The other two are for …" she asks as she looks at us.

"My mom, and the other is for my place," Walker answers.

"Well, your mother's ceiling isn't as high as ours, so I think we'll take the taller one. You and Edith can fight over who gets the fuller one," she says with a smile as she eyeballs me.

"The tall one it is," I say as I pull my gloves on and undo the bungee cord holding the trees in place.

The women back up as Walker and I load their pick onto our shoulders and guide it toward the steps.

Pop holds the door open wide, and we carry the tree to the usual spot at the bay windows that look out to the front of the house.

We secure the tree, and I pull my gloves off before I walk back outside.

Doreen is standing there with her hands on her hips, watching me. "What's wrong?" she asks.

"Nothing."

"Oh, please, Braxton Young. I know when something has you agitated. Is it having to deliver trees? I could have sent Jefferson and Emmett to fetch it."

"No, ma'am. It's not that."

"Then, what is it?" she asks as she and Ria and Pop all stare at me, waiting.

The screen door opens, and Walker comes in behind me, popping the top off a cold beer.

"He's got his panties all in a wad because Sophie's mom and stepdad are coming for Christmas," he spills.

"Is that all?" Ria asks, confused.

"Yep, he is being a big ole baby about the whole thing. He even made Sophie cry."

"Braxton," Doreen scolds.

I cut my eyes to Walker and give him a seething glare, and the asshole just grins at me.

"I'm not in the mood to put up with Vivian. Sophie is exhausted and doesn't need to be playing hostess, and I barely get time with my girls as it is. I wanted our first Christmas together to be special, relaxed, just the three of us enjoying each other," I defend myself.

"Oh, Braxton, don't you think you're being a little selfish?" Ria asks.

"Selfish? No," I retort.

"You can't expect Sophie to turn her parents away. Especially now. Son, when a woman has a baby of her own, she wants and needs her mother," Doreen adds.

"Why? She has you guys and Madeline and Elle. Dallas is an expert."

"That's not the same. She wants her mother. Just like a child wants its mother when it's sick or overwhelmed. Vivian might be a bit overbearing, but she loves Sophie, and Sophie loves her and wants to share this precious time with her. It's a bonding experience. Plus, it's Lily Claire's first Christmas, and Sophie wants her grandmother to be a part of it, just like Gram was a part of all her Christmas memories," Doreen explains.

I hang my head. "Shit, I am an asshole."

Doreen lays her hand on my shoulder. "You're just new to this husband and father thing. You'll get the hang of it. Just talk to her and apologize for overreacting and any other knuckleheaded thing you might have said. Then, offer a compromise. Like, after everything settles on Christmas Day, you and your girls go home together to spend the evening alone. Vivian and Stan can hang out with us or in town. I'm sure they wouldn't mind just one night at the inn."

I look at her and then back up on the porch to Ria and Pop.

"I'm not winning any Happily Married awards, am I?" I ask.

Pop bursts into laughter, and all eyes turn to him.

"Son, there is no such thing. Gram and I were married for over sixty years, and I know a thing or two."

"If I don't get my shit together, I don't think Sophie will put up with me for sixty years."

"Notice I didn't say, I was happily married for sixty years, son. Anyone who claims that is a damn liar. Ain't nobody happy every day for sixty years. I loved Gram with everything I had, but there were some days we could barely stand the sight of each other. That woman could make me madder than a hornet, and she never had a problem letting me know that I could do the same. She locked me out of the house and made me sleep out in the barn on more than one occasion over the years. That woman had a temper. But we loved each other, and we loved our family. The fights were temporary, and the making up was divine."

"Is that right, old man?" I ask.

"Yep. There is no such thing as a perfect union. Marriage is just two flawed individuals who make a choice each day not to give up on each other. That's the beauty of grown-up love. You'll find out that you're more flawed than she is, and she'll be the one not giving up the most because that's the way of a woman in love with an old cowboy. So, buy her lots of flowers and learn to grovel."

"I messed up."

"Then, you be man enough to tell her you're sorry and mean it. Women are built differently than men. We can get angry, yell, and curse awhile, and then we get over it, and everything is fine. But females, it festers with them and settles in like little cracks in their souls. They need the words. So, we have to be man enough to humble ourselves and give them the words. You remember that, and you'll be a fine husband for the next sixty years."

"Damn, I need to be taking notes, don't I?" Walker chimes. "Can you repeat that part about flawed people?" he asks as he pulls his phone from his back pocket and taps the screen.

Pop slaps him on the back. "I don't think there's much hope for you, son. You'd just better pray Elle has the patience of a saint, and it couldn't hurt to go ahead and hide yourself a pillow out in the barn."

"That is solid advice, Pop," Walker agrees.

Doreen just shakes her head and then turns back to me. "Are you sorted?"

"Yes, ma'am." I give in before kissing her cheek.

"Wonderful. Now, let's get in there and get that tree wrapped in lights," she urges Aunt Ria.

They head excitedly into the house, and Pop follows. I shut the tailgate, and Walker and I load up into the truck to head to his mom's house.

I make it home and find Elle on the couch, watching television.

"Hey, big brother," she says as she stretches.

I look around and see that the house is all in order. I can smell dinner cooking in the kitchen, and all the ornaments and decor are laid out in front of the tree, just waiting to deck the halls.

"It looks good in here," I say as I take it all in.

"Yeah, we worked our tails off, trying to get everything done before Vivian and Stanhope arrive. Sophie wanted it all to be just right. Wore herself out."

"Is she in the kitchen?" I ask.

"Nope. The baby woke up hungry about twenty minutes ago, and she went to feed her. I'm keeping an eye on the roast in the oven. Go on and find them and start groveling."

I roll my eyes at her.

"Seriously, Braxton. You hurt her today."

I sigh. "I know. I'll fix it."

"You'd better. Or all the females in your life are going to be angry with you."

I muss her hair, and she growls at me as I head down the hall in search of my girls.

I find them in the nursery. Sophie is in the gliding rocker with Lily Claire in her arms. The baby is latched on to her momma's breast, and Sophie's head is lulled to the side. They are both fast asleep.

She is so beautiful; it takes my breath away. *How the hell did I get so lucky?*

I tiptoe over to them and bend down to kiss Sophie's head and then the baby's. Lily Claire stirs and starts suckling again, which causes one of Sophie's eyes to peek open.

"Hey," she whispers.

"Hey."

"What time is it?"

"It's about three p.m. I just got home."

"Oh, I need to get up. Mom and Stanhope will be here soon," she says as she starts to stand.

"No, you relax. I'll help Elle finish up anything else that needs to be done."

She lets out a sigh and drops back into the rocker. I know she's exhausted.

I take a knee in front of her. "I'm sorry for the way I acted earlier," I begin.

She eyes me suspiciously. "You are?"

I nod. "I know I was a jerk, and you didn't deserve that. Not any of it. It's important for you to have your mom here, isn't it?" I ask.

Her eyes well with tears, and she sniffles as she answers, "Yeah, I know she can be a lot, but something about her presence just calms me. Like I need to be smothered and fussed over right now. The way she has always smothered and fussed over me. I know that doesn't make any sense, but I kind of need her."

I reach up and wipe her tears. "Hey, no need for these. I understand. I'm sorry I got angry. Your parents are welcome here. I promise to be my most charming self."

That gets her to laugh.

"Oh boy, I can't wait to see that."

"You just wait, Princess. I bet you I'll have Vivian eating out of the palm of my hand before next weekend," I inform her.

She gives me a broad smile, and it tugs at my heart.

"No more Mr. Grinch?"

"No more Mr. Grinch. You have my word. We're going to have the best Christmas ever."

"What's the catch?"

"There is no catch, but I do have a request. A compromise. On Christmas Eve, you and I will read *The Night Before Christmas* to Lily Claire before we put her down for the night, and in the morning, we'll all get up and come down to see what Santa left before we head to Rustic Peak for Christmas breakfast. Walker and I'll get work done with Jefferson and Emmett before we come back and open gifts from the family and spend the day with everyone. Your mom and Stanhope included. But after our time with the entire family, we—just the three of us—are coming back here and having a quiet night with the fire going and the tree lit up with us and Hawk on the couch, watching cheesy holiday movies."

She giggles. "You do realize your daughter is two months old, right?"

"I don't care. That's going to be our tradition, and it's starting this year."

Her tears start falling again.

"Is that a no?"

"No! I mean, yes, that sounds like a great plan. I'll make arrangements for Mom and Stan to stay in town Christmas night."

"Then, why are you crying?" I ask as I swipe her hair from her face.

"I'm just so happy at the thought of Lily Claire being surrounded by a large, loud, loving family every Christmas. She's a blessed little one to have so many people who love her."

"Yes, she is. Very loved indeed."

"Sophie?" we hear Elle call down the hallway.

"Yeah, Elle?"

"Do you want me to add the potatoes and carrots to the roast now?"

"Oh, I'm coming. One sec," she answers as she gently pulls the baby from her chest.

Lily Claire grunts in protest.

"You've had plenty. Momma has to go get everyone else's supper ready too, greedy girl," she coos before raising her for me to take.

"I got her," I assure her as she stands and starts for the door.

I reach out and catch her around the waist with one arm as I cradle our daughter in my other arm.

She turns, and I pull her in and kiss her deeply.

"I love you, Sophia Doreen Young," I murmur against her lips.

"I love you more," she says before I release her, and she hurries to the kitchen.

I look down at Lily Claire, and her big blue eyes are watching me.

"Hey, gorgeous. Daddy loves you too," I tell her, and she blinks before tooting loudly.

"What was that? Did that big stinky come out of you, little lady? You are acting like your uncle Walker now," I say as I take over and lay her on the changing table to check her diaper. "Wow, you blew that one up. How did you do that?"

She just gurgles and coos at me as she kicks her chunky legs.

I get her all cleaned up and freshly diapered, and then I remove my shirt before I pick her back up and lay her against my chest, skin to skin. Then, I start walking her around the room, singing softly to her.

"Every time I look into your lovely eyes, I see a love that money just

can't buy. One look from you, I drift away. I pray that you are here to stay. Anything you want, you got it. Anything you need, you got it. Anything at all, you got it, baby …"

I don't know the rest of the lyrics, so I just hum and sway until her eyes grow heavy, and she finally gives in.

I'm not ready to lay her down. I want to hold her a bit longer, so I just close my eyes and continue to hum. When I open them again, I see Sophie leaning against the doorframe, watching us.

"Roy Orbison, huh?" she asks softly.

I shrug. "Not a lullaby kind of guy, but ole Roy got it right. She has me wrapped around her finger, and anything she wants, anything at all, I'll work my ass off to make sure she gets it," I admit.

"I think she has it all right here. Nothing beats being held by your daddy and feeling safe and protected. That's all she needs. At least, until she's a teenager."

"Shit, I don't want to think about that."

She walks over to us and wraps her arms around the two of us. "We'll cross that bridge when it comes."

I pull her in close, and she lays her head on my chest, next to Lily Claire.

"You know, I was worried about how you would do when we found out she was a girl instead of a boy."

"Why? Don't you know, loving girls is my specialty?"

She giggles as I start to dance us around the room.

"I'm truly sorry I was such an ass this morning, Princess. I'm still figuring this husband and father thing out."

"I think you're doing a wonderful job," she whispers.

I kiss her head and start humming again as I twirl my two girls around in the dark.

Three

DALLAS

"MOMMA!" BEAU YELLS FOR ME FROM UPSTAIRS.

"I'm coming!" I call up.

I look to Myer, who is carrying boxes in from the shed.

"When did I go from Mommy to Momma?" I ask.

"A couple of weeks ago."

"Ugh, I don't like it. Soon, it'll be Mom, and then one day, it'll be, *Yo, Dal, can you pack my snacks for football practice?*"

He chuckles as he sets the box on the living room floor.

"It's not funny," I insist.

"Momma, are you coming? I need help. I can't find my boots."

"See, there. You don't have to worry about him growing up too soon. He still needs you," Myer assures me.

"Yeah, like you don't still need me to find your boots," I tease.

He comes over and lifts me off my feet. "That's right. We all need you," he says before he brings his lips to mine.

"Ugh, you guys, stop all the loving. I have to get ready. Nana is going to be here in a minute to get me."

Myer releases me, and we both look to the top of the stairs, where an annoyed, half-dressed Beau stands.

"Sorry, buddy, you know the rules," Myer says as he gestures up to the mistletoe hanging above us.

Beau huffs and comes running down the steps, heading right for us. When he skids to a stop, he reaches up, and Myer plucks him from the floor. Beau wraps his arms around my neck and I take him into my arms as he smacks a kiss right on my lips.

"Now, can we find my boots? I don't want to miss the elves!" he cries.

"Yes, baby, I'll find your boots. Let Daddy comb your hair. I want you to look handsome in the pictures."

I drop him to his bare feet and head up to find his favorite boots. I fish one out of the back of his closet and the other from under his bed.

When I make it back downstairs, Mom is already standing at the door, waiting for him. They will be having cookies and milk with some of Santa's elves down at the church tonight. I hate sending Beau without us, but it's the perfect opportunity for us to get some gifts wrapped and hidden away. Plus, we still have the Poplar Falls tree lighting ceremony this weekend, and Santa will be there, so I'll get pictures of Beau and his baby sister with him then.

"Here you go. You know, if you put them on your shoe rack, where they belong, when you take them off, we wouldn't have to hunt them down every time," I say as I hand them off to Myer, and he helps Beau get them on.

"I know, Mommy. I'm sorry," he says.

Myer's eyes come to mine, and he grins.

I got a *Mommy*. It still slips out from time to time, and I have to savor each one of them when they do.

"It's okay, baby. Next time, you'll remember," I say before I grab his coat and hat.

I pull it on and button him up before I bring him in for a squeeze.

"You have fun and mind Nana and Pop-Pop. I'll see you in the morning before school."

"Okay, I love you," he says before taking my mom's hand.

"We'll get up early and swing by the bakery for breakfast before I drop him off," she says as she leads him out to the truck, where Daddy is waiting.

I stand in the open door and wave until they are out of sight.

Arms come around me from behind, and Myer's chin rests on my head.

"I don't want him to grow up. It's happening too fast. He was a baby yesterday, and now, he's eight years old. I blinked, and he turned into a little man."

"You can't stop time," he whispers into my hair.

"I don't want to stop it. I just want it to slow down," I gripe.

Headlights turn down the drive.

"That's Payne. He is going to help me put the bed together."

We are redoing the bigger guest bedroom upstairs for Beau. We ordered him a new black metal loft frame with steps for him to climb to get into bed and his very own Batman Batcave below, which holds a desk and TV with a Loki beanbag chair. Captain America's shield is painted on the ceiling with a star-shaped light fixture in the center. The opposite wall of the built-in bed is painted to look like bricks with a huge Incredible Hulk fist busting through it. I had metal letters made that spell out his name and the words *Hero Up*. Plus, Santa is bringing him all-new Avengers bedding. He is going to freak out. The trick is to keep him from seeing it before Christmas. He never goes in there, but I'm terrified he'll wander in for some reason between now and then.

"Is the little man gone?" Payne asks as he climbs the steps to the porch.

"Yes, Momma and Daddy just picked him up."

"Let's get to it, then," he says as he follows me inside.

"I brought the boxes in already. It looks like this thing is in a million pieces, so it should be a lot of fun to put it together," Myer tells him.

"Bring it on. I love a challenge."

"I'll get supper done while y'all work," I tell them before heading to the kitchen.

Three hours later, they emerge from upstairs.

"I'd ask how it went, but I heard a plethora of curses coming from up there," I say as the two of them settle into barstools.

"Jeez, they couldn't have made that thing harder to assemble. But we finally beat it into submission. It looks good. Beau's going to love it," Payne informs.

"I'll go check it out and lock the door before I go to bed. I don't want Beau to see it and ruin the surprise. By the way, do you want us to wait for you to get here on Christmas morning before we show it to him? You should get to see his face since you worked so hard on it even though Santa gets all the credit."

"I wanted to talk to you about that," he says.

I dish out lasagna and pile their plates high and add a piece of garlic bread before sliding it in front of them.

"All right, shoot," I prompt him.

"I'm going to New York for Christmas," he says.

"What?"

"I want to surprise Charlotte. She keeps hinting that she wants something big for Christmas, and I can't think of anything to get her, so I figure I'll give her me."

"You, in New York City, at Christmas?" I burst into laughter.

"Nice," he grumbles.

"I'm sorry. I'm just trying to picture it," I say as I continue to laugh.

He sits back and waits for me to get my wits about me.

"You done?" he asks impatiently.

I take a deep breath. "Yep, I think so."

"I know Mom is going to give me a hard time, but Christmas weekend is the only time I can be away from the farm for a few days. I'll be back the day after Christmas, and we can all get together then," he suggests.

"Works for me, but I can't wait for you to show Beau his room. I'll record him for you though, or you can call, and you and Charlotte can watch on FaceTime."

We hear a whine through the monitor, and I start for our room, but Myer stands.

"I'll get her," he says.

I turn back to my brother. "So, New York ... that's kind of a big deal, don't you think?"

"No bigger deal than her coming here."

"Oh, yes, it is. She comes here to see Sophie, me, and Elle, and you are in the mix somewhere. But you going to New York, where you do not know another soul? It's all kinds of different."

"I just miss her crazy ass. I haven't seen her since the weekend Faith was born. She's been so busy with all the holiday sales and shit, and with Sophie not being able to fly there, she hasn't been able to get away. I figure she's the one always taking on the trouble and expense to come to me. It's only fair I make an effort and go to her."

"Uh-huh," I say as I take a sip from my tea glass.

He shakes his head at the scrutiny. "Just help me with Mom, will you? Pretty please, sis?"

"All right. I'll handle her. She likes Charlotte even if she does think she's a tad kooky. She'll be fine."

"Thanks."

Myer comes back with Faith in his arms and Cowboy, Beau's dog, on his heels.

"Well, hello, sleeping beauty. I was wondering if you planned on joining us this evening." I reach for her. "Let me have her. I'll feed her while you finish eating."

He passes our daughter off to me, and I walk to the living room to feed her.

I started back to work at the bakery I own with my mother last week, and it has killed me to leave her with my mother-in-law every morning. I know she's in good hands, but I miss her. Dealing with those emotions is probably contributing to me being so fragile about Beau growing up. I don't want to miss a single thing. Time really is like sands through the hourglass.

The boys finish their meal, and after he sees Payne off, Myer joins us on the couch.

I hand the baby off to her daddy, and then I pull my feet up and curl into his side.

"It's starting to snow out," he informs me.

"That's good. Beau will be happy if it sticks. He's been dying to go sledding."

"What about you? I seem to remember you getting awfully excited about sledding yourself."

"Not this year. Faith is too little, and the last thing we need is for one of us to hurt ourselves right now. The only sledding I'd be up for is a ride on Santa's sleigh," I manage before a huge yawn escapes me.

"Ready for bed?" he asks.

I shake my head. "No. I just want to lie here in front of the fire and watch the tree twinkle a little while longer."

He pulls me in closer, and I lay my head in his lap as he holds a sleeping Faith tucked into the opposite side.

Cowboy hops up and settles on my feet.

I drift off to sleep five minutes later.

Four

MYER

"I'M SORRY I'M RUNNING LATE. I OVERSLEPT, AND FAITH JUST finished feeding. I'll be there in fifteen," Dallas says into the phone.

I get Faith fastened safely into her car seat as she grabs her coat and keys.

We walk out together, and I secure the car seat to the base in my truck. Dallas stands behind me to give the baby one last kiss before I shut her in.

I turn and wrap her in my arms.

"It'll get easier," I assure her as she stands there, about to cry.

"Will it?" she asks.

"I promise. She's only four months old, and you've been back to work for less than a month."

"I miss her when I'm there," she says. "When Beau was this little, we lived with my parents, and I was home with him until he started preschool. It feels wrong."

It is the same conversation we have every morning.

"Dal, baby, if you want to stay home until she's in school or just until you are ready, you can. You don't have to work. We'll make it. You know that, right?"

She nods.

"It's my bakery. I kind of have to be there," she says.

"I'm sure your mom could handle it a few more months."

"No, that's not fair. Faith is perfectly happy and well cared for by your momma. I'm just being a girl," she declares as she wipes her eyes and finds her resolve.

"Okay, then get your ass in your truck and go get your shop open before your morning customers looking for their coffee and muffin fix revolt," I say as I release her and give her a little push.

She turns and mopes all the way to the driver's door, and I open it for her.

"I'll bring you lunch when I come by during my break," she offers.

"Sounds good. Be careful driving with the snow coming in," I remind her before I lean into the door and kiss her.

I wait for her to pull out, and then I get in my truck, so Faith and I can head to Stoney Ridge.

I walk into Mom and Pop's house, holding Faith's car seat in one hand and the diaper bag Dallas packed in the other.

Pop comes down the hall. "Is that my granddaughter?" he asks.

It's the same thing every morning.

"It is," I say as I unfasten her and pick her up.

I hand her off, and Pop walks over to the rocking recliner and sits with her. He clicks on the television to his morning news program and rocks Faith while he watches.

I unpack the bag and put the bottles in the fridge.

"Good morning, sweetheart," Mom says as she walks in, still in her housecoat.

"Morning."

"I see your father is already hogging the baby again," she grumbles.

"He's teaching her current affairs."

She starts the coffeepot and turns to me. "Would you like me to scramble you some eggs or something before you guys get to work?"

"Dallas fed me before we left. I could use your help with something though."

"What's that, dear?"

"Do you still have that old carriage stored somewhere?"

"The one your uncle used to use as a prop when he ran the Christmas tree lot?"

"Yeah, what happened to it?"

"I think it's still in the old storage building out on his property. What in the world made you think of that thing?"

"I want to fix it up. Sand it, paint it, and fit it with a hitch, so a couple of our horses could pull it in the snow. Maybe add some sleigh bells."

"What for?"

"Dallas mentioned that she would like to take a ride in Santa's sleigh. I thought I could do the next best thing as a surprise for her and Beau."

"That's a wonderful idea. That old thing is just sitting there, rotting," she says.

"I'll help you, son. Foster and Truett can haul it out to the barn, and we can put it in the back. I bet with the four of us, it won't take long," Pop offers.

"I'd appreciate that. I'd like to surprise them before we come to have Christmas Eve dinner here."

"Then, I guess you should hand over that baby, so you fellas can get a move on," Momma says as she hurries over to Pop with her hands out.

"She doesn't want you. She wants her grandpoppy," Pop snaps as he holds Faith out of her reach.

"Winston Wilson, you hand her over this instant," Momma huffs.

He looks down at Faith, who is blowing bubbles as she coos at them.

"I'm going to give your grammy a turn, so she doesn't start crying, but Grandpoppy will be back soon, and we'll watch the evening news together."

Momma looks to me and rolls her eyes.

We spend the morning and afternoon moving the cattle to the winter pasture. Most of our part-time staff are on leave the months of December through March, so it's just Pop, Foster, Truett, and me. We lose sunlight pretty early this time of year, so our workdays are much shorter.

After we finish, Foster and I drive out to my uncle's property; he left it to Mom. We load the old carriage onto one of our trailers.

"This thing sure has seen better days," Foster muses.

It is in bad disrepair. This might have been a bad idea.

"Maybe I overshot my expectation. It was just an old prop, not a working carriage," I admit.

"Nah, it's got the bones. We can do an addition. Add some seating and the hitch. A little sanding, some quality paint, and we can make it a beauty. Might need a few more hands if you want it by Christmas Eve though."

"Let's get it back to the ranch and get a better look at it. If we think it's possible, I'll talk to some of the other guys and see if they have time to lend a hand. It can't hurt to ask," I agree.

When we make it back, Pop and Truett are waiting. They help us unload it and get it in the back of the barn.

"What a hunk of junk," Truett proclaims.

"You have to see its potential, son," Pop counters.

Truett lets out a slow whistle. "We'd be better off starting from scratch and building one ourselves."

"Nah, this one has history, and it just needs some TLC," Foster declares.

"All right, if you say so. Let's give it a go." Truett gives in.

I explain how I'd like to add two facing benches with cushioned seats, so they will be comfortable. A driver's seat with a sturdy hitch to hold at least a couple of horses.

"I want to paint it a Christmas red and trim it in gold or silver. Dallas and Beau will love it," I tell them.

"Okay, okay, I can see it. We'll have to cut it in two and extend it to get the seats in. Foster and I should be able to put a hitch together for you. We have a welder down at Gramps's, and he has a pile of scrap metal. I'm sure he won't mind if we use some of it," Truett says as he walks around the carriage and looks under the front end.

We hear a vehicle pulling down the drive, and Pop looks out.

"That's your bride now."

I look down at my watch. It's past seven.

"Dammit, I lost track of time. I was supposed to be home by now," I confess as I grab a rag and wipe my hands.

"Go on, before she comes looking for you. We'll get this thing covered, and we'll start working on it tomorrow," Pop insists.

"We'll start on the welding tonight," Foster says.

"Thanks, guys. I truly appreciate it."

I jog out to greet Dallas and Beau, and they head to the house.

"I'm sorry, Dal. We started working on one of the tractors, and I lost track of time."

"It's fine. I called Beverly, and she was running low on bottles. I should probably start pumping more and freezing it."

"Can I ride Bolt?" Beau asks.

"Not tonight, baby," Dallas says.

"Please, Momma?"

"We have to get home and eat supper and do your homework before bath and bedtime," she tells him.

"I'm not hungry," he complains.

"Don't back-talk your mother," I correct him.

"I'm sorry, Momma," he mumbles.

"Sorry, baby. I know we've been crazy busy the past few months, and I've been extra tired because of your sister." She soothes him as she runs her fingers through his hair.

"It's okay," he tells her.

He loves his baby sister, and he has been very patient and a big help around the house.

"Tell you what, buddy. You get two weeks off for your Christmas break, and you can come to work with me if you want. You can help me and Pop out on the ranch, and you and I will get as much riding time in as possible. If Santa comes through with that new dirt bike you put on your list, we can even clear a corral, so you can practice riding it."

"Really? Can Uncle Payne come?"

"Sure."

"Cool. Thanks, Dad!" he exclaims before he runs up the porch.

"You were right," I tell Dallas as I hook my arm around her neck and lead her into the house.

"About what?"

AMBER KELLY

"I've gone from Daddy to Dad overnight, and it stings," I admit.

"I know, right?!"

"At least we have Faith to count on to keep us feeling young and important," I tell her, and she laughs.

"Are you saying I'm going to have to keep popping out babies, so we aren't phased out?" she asks.

I curl her into me. "Now, that sounds like a good plan."

She wraps her arms around my waist. "I bet it does to you. Your part in the deal is all fun and no swollen ankles or added stretch marks."

"I can make it fun for you too," I say before I kiss her neck.

She sighs. "And those stretch marks are sexy as hell."

The door swings wide.

"Are y'all kissing again?" Beau asks.

"You know the rules, buddy," I say.

He looks up.

"I don't see no mistletoe," he protests.

"I don't see *any* mistletoe," Dallas corrects.

I reach in my shirt pocket for the sprig of mistletoe I stashed there and hold it above Dallas's head.

Beau huffs out an exasperated breath and walks out on the porch. He reaches his arms out, and I grab him up. He plants a kiss on his momma's lips, and then he turns to me.

"You'd better hide that stuff before Christmas Eve. Mrs. Gaddis taught us a song today. Santa likes to kiss mommies if there is mistletoe hanging, and you have it all over the place. If he is in the house and Momma gets up to feed Faith, he's going to lay one on her for sure."

With that, he slides down and races back inside.

Dallas goes to follow him, and I whisper in her ear, "Oh, Santa plans on kissing every inch of Mommy on Christmas night."

Five

ELOWYN

"**E**LLE, THIS PLACE IS SO FREAKING COOL," BELLAMY SAYS as she looks around.

Walker and the guys completed our home build last month. He and I have started furnishing it, and he is settling in. I'm still at Rustic Peak until our wedding this spring, much to his chagrin. He was ready for me to move in yesterday, but I want to wait. It just adds an extra layer of excitement to our wedding day.

Bellamy and Sonia are here today, helping me unpack some of the things Aunt Doreen and Aunt Ria gifted us for the kitchen. Then, we will rearrange the furniture that Walker and Braxton just haphazardly scattered around the ample, open living space.

"It is amazing. Better than I envisioned when we came up with the plans," I agree.

"Not going to lie. I'm a little bit jealous," Bellamy admits as she begins hanging the copper pots above the kitchen island.

"You? You are living in our dream house," Sonia interjects.

Bellamy moved into the old Sugarman Homestead right outside of downtown with her fiancé, Dr. Brandt Haralson, Poplar Falls' new vet. It is a historic old manor that he purchased and renovated. We had fantasized about living in the gigantic house since we were little girls. Brandt turned it into a sleek, modern dream home for her.

"If anyone should be jealous, it's me. I'm the one still living in a seven-hundred-square-foot, one-bedroom apartment above my mother's consignment shop," Sonia adds.

"That apartment is super nice and fits your lifestyle perfectly. You're on Main Street, just steps away from shopping, coffee, baked goods, and restaurants. Everything a girl needs," I tell her.

"Yeah, it's a real dream come true," Sonia retorts as she rolls her eyes.

"Stop that right now. You were thrilled when your mother let you move into that apartment. We all were. We still lived at home, and you had your own space," Bellamy says.

Sonia sighs. "I know. I guess I'm still bitter because Ricky and I were looking at houses, and I had my heart set on that charming log cabin near Stoney Ridge. It was perfect, and I got my hopes up," she admits.

"Why don't you try to buy it on your own? You have a great career and make your own money. It's not like Ricky was financially contributing that much," I suggest.

"I can't do anything until the divorce is final. I don't want to buy something, only to have to split it with him. I mean, I don't think he'd sink that low, but I don't want to assume anything anymore, and I doubt the place will still be available next summer," she says, the disappointment rolling off her.

I hate that her marriage fell apart in under a year. She had been so happy on her wedding day, and even though none of us were Ricky's biggest fan, we all hoped he was turning a corner for her.

"That just means that there is another home out there for you, and you're going to love it even more," Bellamy encourages.

"Yeah, maybe," Sonia says as she turns and walks into the living space, where she starts to shuffle through another box.

I look at Bellamy, and she slightly nods her head. We don't like seeing our perky, optimistic friend so down. She's the best of us. A wonderful friend and a caregiver. Oh, how we wish she had someone in her life to care for her the way she cares for others.

"How is the party planning coming along?" I ask Bellamy.

"We're almost done. The renovations are complete, thank goodness, and Momma and Pop are coming to help us decorate tomorrow night. So, barring anything major, we should be ready by Thursday."

"Do you need any help?" I offer.

"Nope. I don't want anyone lifting a finger. No cooking, no cleaning, and I don't want you to bring a single thing. We have a stocked bar, and Dallas and her mother are catering. We hired a cleanup crew for the next morning. If you drink too much, we have three empty guest rooms that you are welcome to claim," she says.

"Are you sure? I'd be more than happy to bring something."

She shakes her head. "It's our Christmas gift to all our friends. We just want everyone to get dressed up and enjoy the evening."

"Okay, if you insist." I give in.

"That goes for you too. I already claimed one of the rooms for you. You're staying the night," she calls to Sonia.

"Sounds good to me, especially if Dallas's mom is making her famous eggnog. I'll be happy not to have to drive."

"Oh, there will be eggnog for sure."

We continue to work, and once everything in the kitchen is put away, we move to the furniture.

"I'm thinking the L-shaped leather sofa should go here, facing the fireplace. I wanted to hang a piece of art above it, but Walker purchased that insanely large television, and there is nowhere else the thing will fit, except above the mantel. So, all the sitting spaces need to face it," I instruct.

"Let's get your cowhide rug down first and then move the couch. Are you going to put a coffee table in here?" Bellamy asks.

"Yes, Uncle Jefferson and Pop are making me one to match the farmhouse dining room table they are building as our wedding gift. So, that will be a while."

We get the rug laid out, and we all grab an edge of the couch to start moving it.

Bellamy grunts as she tries to get a good handle on the leather and lifts.

Sonia drops her end just as I lift my corner up.

"Sorry," she says before bending back down to pick it up again. "It's a slippery sucker."

We get it moved a couple of steps when the front door swings open.

"Whoa, what are you women doing?" Walker asks as he and Silas come in, toting a Christmas tree.

"Decorating," I say as I blow a piece of hair from my face.

"Put that thing down," he commands.

We slowly lower it and drop it to the floor.

"What?" I ask as he and Silas set the tree in the stand by the front window, and he walks to me.

"You're going to hurt yourselves. It's heavy. Si and I will get it," he says before he grabs me and kisses me hard.

"Gross," Bellamy exclaims.

He lets me go, turns his head, and points at her. "Don't make me come lay one on you, woman," he threatens.

Bellamy throws her hands in the air and backs up.

"Are you finished for the day?" I ask him.

"Yep, this was the last stop. So, if you want to decorate the tree tonight, we can. I can throw some steaks on the grill for dinner," he says.

"We can string up the lights, but I planned to buy all the ornaments and things we need at the Christmas Market this weekend during the tree lighting. I only have a couple of sentimental ones that

Aunt Madeline saved for me from Momma's collection when they packed up the house, and I'm assuming you don't have any."

"Nope. This is my first official Christmas tree." He grins.

"Our first official tree, you mean," I correct him.

He shakes his head. "Nope. It's mine. If you want to claim the tree, you have to move in," he teases.

I fake a pout.

"That's not going to work, woman. Tuck that bottom lip back in."

"But—"

"But nothing," he cuts me off. "You move your ass in, or it's all mine."

"I told you, I'm not moving in until—"

"Until the wedding. I know. So, let's go down to the courthouse and get a license, and we'll get married this weekend. We can get married in the middle of the Christmas Market. Everyone will be there. It's perfect."

I push against his chest, but he doesn't let me escape.

"I'm serious. I can have Reverend Burr there, and we'll say *I do* in front of the whole damn town," he says, all joking aside.

"Uh-uh. I told you, I want a church wedding. It doesn't have to be big. I've always wanted to get married in the same small church where my momma married my daddy. Wearing her dress with Braxton walking me down the aisle."

His eyes soften, and he leans his forehead against mine.

"It's always been my dream," I whisper against his lips.

"Woman, I'd marry you anywhere, anytime, and if you want to get married in that church, then we will get married in that church. It'd better be soon though; a man only has so much patience when he's waiting for a beautiful woman to start sleeping beside him every night."

I shake my head as tears of disappointment start to leak from my eyes.

"Ah, no, no, no crying. I was just kidding. I have the patience of a saint when it comes to you. I can wait as long as you want me to." He backtracks.

I shake my head. "It's not that. Sonia and I rode out there last week. To the church, I mean. It looks to be in severe disrepair. I talked to one of the guys who lives across the street, and he said the church outgrew the space. They purchased property a couple miles down the road and built a bigger facility a few years ago. They donated the land, where the original one stood, to the community. The chapel was broken into by vandals, so they had to board it up. They're planning to tear it down and build a playground for the surrounding neighborhood."

He sighs. "I'm sorry, Elle. We can always get married at their new building. It's the same church, just a different address." He gives an alternative.

I look up at him, nod, and wipe at my cheeks.

"It's not the same, is it?" he asks as he kisses the top of my head.

"It's close enough. I did call to see what their schedule looks like for the spring at the new location and they are booked solid until November."

"The end of the year? I can't wait that long. Why don't you let me pay them a visit and see what I can do?" he offers.

I pull back and give him a *yeah, right* look.

"Hey, you have finals to worry about and are helping Doe and Ria with Christmas meal prep and Bells with that gala thing. Your plate is full. I can handle this one thing. Promise." He crosses his heart.

I ponder it for a moment.

"Okay. It was Saint Mary's Chapel, but I think they are called Saint Mary's Baptist Church now. Just make sure to let them know we will have our own officiant and our own music and that we would like to just rent the venue. Any Saturday in February or early March would be ideal, but most churches book up way in advance, so they could be full until later in the year. If so, we'll have to figure something else out, or you will just have to wait."

"They'll have something in February," he growls.

I stick my finger in his chest and tap as I speak, "No bullying the church folks, Walker Reid. I'm trusting you."

He grins.

"I mean it!"

"Yes, ma'am," he says before he smacks my behind. "Now that that's settled, go get me a beer, woman, so we can get this couch moved."

I give him the stink eye. Then, I walk slowly past him.

"I'm getting you a beer only because I want to and because Silas looks thirsty," I say.

I motion to the kitchen with my head, and the girls follow me.

"I'm glad they showed up when they did. He's right; that thing is heavy," Sonia says before she and Bellamy plop into the seats at the island.

I take out a bottle opener and pop the tops off two cold ones before returning to the living room and setting them on the mantel. Then, I show the boys exactly where I want the couch before I walk back to the kitchen and open bottles for us girls.

"I can't believe you are letting Walker handle any part of the wedding," Bellamy says.

"Eh, if he fails, it's no big deal. Maybe I should just get married at Gram's church and be happy. It's not like my parents are here to care where it happens."

Bellamy lays her hand on top of mine. "You care, and it's your day. I hate that you might have to compromise."

"Me too, but at least I'm marrying a man I love more than anything, and that's one thing I do have in common with Momma."

"I'll drink to that," Bellamy says as we lift our bottles in the air and clink.

Six

WALKER

"I'M HEADING OUT EARLY TODAY," I YELL TO JEFFERSON AND Braxton as I take off my muddy work boots in the barn.

"Slacker," Braxton calls.

"I ran circles around you today, Daddy. That baby keeping you up all night or what?"

"In your dreams, Walk."

Jefferson leads his horse to the brushing station. "Where you off to, son?" he asks as he starts removing his saddle.

"Elle has her heart set on a certain church for the wedding. I'm going to go talk to the preacher man and see if I can get a weekend nailed down before next Christmas," I tell him.

"Next Christmas?"

"Yes, sir. Apparently, she called, and they are pretty booked. I'm hoping my charm will persuade them to find us a spot."

He stops and faces me. "You think you're going to sweet-talk a pastor into bumping someone else's wedding day for you? That's a stretch, son."

I sigh. "Hell, I know it is, but Elle has her heart set on that place, and I've got to at least try for her. You should have seen the look on her face when she told me. I'd grovel to anyone not to see her that brokenhearted again."

He nods. "Well, good luck. I hope the Lord finds a way for you."

On my way to the truck, I say a little prayer, "Lord, it's me. I know I'm your problem child, and you wish I'd get my shit … er, stuff together. I'm trying. I truly am. I hate to ask you for favors. You probably think that's the only time you hear from me. But this one isn't for me. It's for Elle, and we both know I might not deserve your help, but she sure does. If there's anything you can do to get us a wedding in this church ASAP, I will be eternally grateful."

It takes twenty minutes to drive out to Saint Mary's. The entire time, I practice what I'm going to say. I want to sound sincere and not demanding, but even I can see this ending with me either begging or stomping off, cursing up a storm.

I park in front of the office building to the side of the sanctuary and step out. It sure is a beautiful church, and the grounds are gorgeous. I bet in the spring, it will be stunning. I can picture Elle in her dress, walking up those steps and smiling from ear to ear with Sonia and Bellamy fussing over her.

I walk over to the door that says *Pastoral Offices* and knock.

A wisp of a man with silver hair and kind eyes opens it.

"You must be Mr. Reid," he greets.

"Yes, sir. You can call me Walker."

"It's nice to meet you, Walker. Please come in," he invites me as he steps aside.

We walk down a narrow hallway to his office, and instead of taking the seat behind his desk, he leads us over to a sofa on the far wall, and we both sit.

"What can I help you with, son?" he asks.

"I'm looking to book your church for my wedding."

His eyebrows rise in surprise. "Is that all? You could have contacted the church secretary and made those arrangements."

I shake my head. "My bride-to-be tried that route. Seems you're all full until next November."

"I see," he says hesitantly.

"Look, I know it's a long shot, but my girl's mother and father were married in your church over forty years ago. She has her heart set on getting married where they did. It's important to her, and that makes it important to me."

"Forty years? That must have been in the chapel down the way."

"It was. That's where she truly wanted to get married, but we know that one is closed. This location is the next best thing."

He sits back and considers me. "Are you willing to do a weekday ceremony?"

"We prefer Saturday. I work on a cattle ranch, and so do eighty percent of the guest list. A Saturday evening would make it a lot easier."

"I'm sorry, Walker, but I can't just take a day away from another couple and give it to you. I wish I could. If your bride's wishes are that important to you, why don't you postpone until the end of the year?"

I hang my head.

Lord, I could really use that backup now.

"Don't think I can wait that long, Pastor."

"It's too bad that old chapel is in such disrepair," he comments.

I lift my head as a crazy idea hits me.

"How bad are we talking? The state of the old chapel, that is," I ask.

"It was vandalized a few months back. They broke one of the stained glass windows. Spray-painted the wall behind the altar. We boarded everything up after that. We donated the wooden pews to a new church in Aurora, and the floor was damaged when they re-moved them. We plan to salvage the remaining stained glass and the altar before it's bulldozed," he explains.

"When is that scheduled?"

"As soon as we raise funds. The account is building, but we don't want to start the project and have the kids waiting for the completion forever, so we're not beginning until we have all we need."

I let the information roll around in my head for a moment and then form a plan.

"What if you didn't tear it down?"

"Come again?"

"Hear me out, Pastor. What if I go in, redo the floor, paint the walls, repair the window, and in return, you let us use the chapel for our wedding? Afterward, the community can use it as a recreation room for the children at the park or a space that it can rent for parties or gatherings. I'll even build them some picnic tables for the inside," I offer.

"I never thought of that," he admits.

"The rent could help keep the park up. Maintenance and lawn care can get pricey. I'll even get some of my friends to volunteer their time, and we'll get some tractors out there to clear the land for the playground equipment."

He ponders my suggestions.

"That's not a horrible idea. The chapel has restrooms and a small kitchenette. That could keep us from having to build new bathroom facilities. When do you propose you could start working on this project?"

"Right after Christmas. We'll work nights and weekends."

"I suppose we could get the electricity and water put back on at the first of the year. There is also a leak in the roof near the steeple," he says with a lift of an eyebrow.

I chuckle. "We can take care of that as well," I offer.

He stands. "I have to make a few phone calls before I can agree to anything. All the church board members have to give approval."

"One more thing, Pastor. If you could hang a plaque in the chapel that reads *Dedicated to the Memory of Tyrone and Lily Young*, I'll even donate all the materials we need for the project. No cost to the church. You can use all the money you've raised for the playground equipment."

"Tyrone and Lily?" He sits back down. "Son, are you marrying Lily's little girl, Elowyn?" he asks.

"Yes, sir."

"I married her parents. I was a new pastor back then. Their wedding was the first I officiated. Tragic, what happened to them. I can't believe that little Elowyn is getting married."

What are the odds?

"We have our reverend, but if you could, it'd mean the world to Elle and Braxton if you were a part of the ceremony," I say hopefully.

"I'd be honored." He stands again. "Now, let me go get everyone on board for this. Your bride will get her wish," he says before walking to the desk and picking up the phone.

When I make it home, the lights are on, and I know that Elle is there. I like this, coming home to her.

I park the truck and climb the porch, and Woof is perched behind the tree with his nose to the window.

I open the door, and he comes barreling to greet me. I bend to scratch him behind his ear.

"You'd better be careful, buddy. You go knocking that tree over, and your mom is going to tan your hide."

I stand and go in search of my girl. I follow the sound of water and ascend the staircase to the loft. A sexy, silky little red number is hanging on the back of the bedroom door, and steam is streaming out of the master bath.

I kick my boots off and shrug out of my shirt as I make my way to join her.

Elle is in the shower, standing under the spray, washing her hair. The glass is foggy, but it affords me the pleasure of a small clear window, so I can appreciate her backside.

I open the door and walk in behind her. She lets out a yelp of surprise as I run my hands down her slick, soapy sides. She relaxes and takes a step back into me.

"Hey," I say into her ear.

"Hey. I was getting worried you were going to be late," she says.

"That's why I'm here. Showering together will save us some time."

She laughs. "That's not how it usually works," she says as she looks over her shoulder at me.

"I'll be good," I promise her, even as my growing erection presses into her.

"Don't be good," she says as her hand snakes around and strokes me.

I growl, "All right, woman, just remember you started it when we're rushing to the party." I turn her to face me and fist my hand in her wet hair.

"You're the one who invaded my shower," she points out.

"Right," I say before I guide her mouth to mine.

Her hands come to my shoulders, and she rises on her tiptoes to meet my kiss. Taut nipples graze my chest, and I tear my mouth from hers to lick a trail down to one rosy bud. I take it between my teeth and bite down.

She jumps into my arms, and my tongue darts out to soothe the peak before I suck it into my mouth again. I give her other breast the same attention before she grabs a handful of my hair and pulls me up. She pushes against me to back me up out of the water, and then she turns us, so her back is against the smooth glass. I take that as an invitation to pick her up, but she halts me. Looking down between us, she takes my erection into her hand and starts to pump her fist around me. I plant my hands above her head and lean my forehead against the glass. Then, my girl slides down the glass to her knees. She wraps her lips around the head of my throbbing cock and slowly takes me into her mouth. Her eyes never leave mine. Damn, this woman can bring me to my knees. I moan as her teeth nibble my sensitive skin. Her hand is working me as she sucks me deeper and deeper.

"Baby," I manage to murmur as the rhythm of her hand and mouth drive me to the edge.

I close my eyes and let the sensation rocket down my spine, drawing my balls tight.

"Elle, I'm going to come, baby," I warn, but she doesn't ease up.

Instead, she quickens her pace, and I try to hold out. Not ready to end this, but I can't control it. I call her name on a roar as I spill into her mouth. She stays on her knees until I'm completely spent. I reach down, pick her up, and kiss her deeply.

"You drive me crazy," I tell her as I kiss her cheeks, her eyes, her nose.

"Come on. We have to finish up, or we're going to be late." She tries to hurry around me, back to the spray, and I stop her.

"Uh-uh, it's your turn," I say before I turn her around to face the back of the shower and press her against the glass.

"Walker, we don't have time," she starts as I pull her hips forward and use my foot to spread her legs.

As soon as my fingers slide around to find her slick and ready, her words die, and she throws her head back against me.

I pinch her clit, and her body bucks.

"That's my good girl," I say as I sink my teeth into her collar.

I find her opening and start pumping one finger in and out. I curl it inside her and find that spot that I know makes her wild. I feel her spasms, and I know she's close.

"Yes, Walker, right there," she encourages me.

I add another finger and bring my thumb up to press in and run circles around her clit. She braces against the shower and starts riding my hand until she explodes. I hold her as her body quakes from her release. When the last tremble shoots through her, she goes limp against my chest.

"Oh no, you don't. We have to hurry," I say as I turn her into the water. "You're going to make us late, woman."

Seven

BELLAMY

"**H**ow do I look?" I ask as I twirl for Brandt.

"Like I want to lock the door, turn out all the lights so everyone thinks we're not home, and peel that dress off of you."

"Awesome. That's just what I was going for," I say as I wrap my arms around him.

"How much time do we have?" he asks.

"About half an hour," I say.

He starts walking us backward toward the bed.

"Brandt, that's not enough time."

"Sure it is," he says as he brushes my hair off one shoulder and starts to run his mouth up my throat.

He knows how much I like that.

"You're going to mess up my makeup," I whine.

"Don't care," he says as he makes it to my mouth.

His hands run up into my hair as he tilts my head to get better access.

"And my hair," I complain.

He kisses me deeply, and I melt into him. All thoughts of my appearance fly right out of my mind as his hand slides up my thigh, fingering the lace at the top of my garters.

"I like these," he growls.

"I know. That's why I wore them."

"To tease me all night?"

"Yep," I say as I arch into his touch, "but just until everyone leaves. Then, you can take them off of me—or not. Whichever you prefer, Doc."

"I need a preview," he demands as he sits on the edge of the bed and pulls my hips to him.

I straddle his legs, and he raises the hem of my dress and kisses the inside of my thigh as his hands come around and palm my ass.

I thread my fingers into his hair as he kisses me through the lace of my panties.

I moan.

That's when the doorbell rings.

"Ugh," he murmurs as he lets my hem down.

"To be continued," I tell him. "Get dressed!"

I step away and adjust my dress before heading to answer the door.

"Do I have to wear a tie?"

"Nope. Walker and Myer will probably show up in jeans and boots."

"I just thought, with you looking so ravishing, you might be expecting everyone to dress to the nines."

I shrug. "We don't get many occasions to pull out our fancy duds, so us girls decided to get dolled up."

"Mmm, lucky us," he says as he crosses the room and catches me. He lays one last kiss on that spot right below my ear that he knows drives me mad.

I push at his chest. "Oh no, you don't."

We hear the doorbell ring again.

"That will be Dottie and Marvin with the food. I'll go let them in, and you finish getting ready," I command as I rush past him and down the staircase.

Back when we were just friends and I found out Brandt had purchased this house, he jokingly promised me that he would have a ballroom added for us girls to throw posh holiday parties. I bet he regrets that right about now because I planned just that. This home was made for entertaining, and I have been dying to play hostess since we moved in.

I peek outside and see Dallas's parents unloading. I open the door and step out to greet them.

"Hi, Dottie. You are right on time."

She has her arms full as she comes up the steps, so I prop the door open and hurry to help her.

"Thank you, Bellamy," she says as I take a box from the top of her pile.

She walks in, and I guide her to the kitchen, where she begins setting up as Marvin carries in the rest of the spread.

"Do you need me to stay and serve?" she asks.

"No, ma'am. I hired Pete, one of Butch's off-duty bartenders, to man the bar, and his girlfriend and her sister are coming to keep everything stocked and refilled on the buffet. They're also doing cleanup."

"Bells!" we hear Sonia's voice from the foyer.

"In the kitchen," I call to her.

She walks in, wearing a gorgeous emerald-green cocktail dress, and her hair is in long, flowing curls.

"Wow, you look amazing." Dottie admires her.

"Thank you. Momma made the dress. I love how it floats," she says as she twirls, and the hem of the dress flows out around her. "I'm going to go drop my bag upstairs, and then I'll come help. Which room is mine for the night?" Sonia asks.

"The first one on the right. The gray and white room."

Brandt follows Marvin in with another load.

"Bellamy, those need to be refrigerated, dear, and added to these dishes here right before people begin to arrive. There is extra shrimp in the cooler as well. The cocktail sauce for the shrimp and the horseradish cream for the roast beef is also in there. I sliced lemon wedges for you, and they are in a Ziplock bag. I did extra in case your bartender needs them too," Dottie instructs.

"Can you stay until the servers arrive? I don't want to forget anything, so I want them to hear this as well. They should be here in about ten minutes or so."

"Of course," she agrees.

Sonia reappears. "What can I do to help?" she asks.

"You can help me get all the trees and candles lit, please." I accept her offer.

We have six Christmas trees. One in almost every room. The outside of the house is trimmed with icicle lights, and all the trees lining the long driveway are lit up as well.

"The band will be here soon, and they will be setting up on the veranda. I hope the heaters we got keep them warm. I didn't realize we'd be getting flurries today. I'd move them inside, but I want everyone to be able to carry on a conversation. If it gets bad, we can move them to the sunroom. We can dance out there as well." I give her the rundown as we go through each room, illuminating it.

"You guys went all out."

"I want this to be our new tradition every year—something for all our friends and us to look forward to," I admit.

"I love that idea," she agrees.

"Hey, did somebody order ice?" Myer's voice comes from downstairs.

"Yes, coming!" I yell down to him.

We finish in the guest rooms and descend the stairs, and he and Braxton are standing there, each with four bags stacked in their arms.

"Let's set them over at the bar. Brandt and Pete can decide where to put it all," I tell them.

They walk into the den and set the bags on the bar.

"Thank you. You're a lifesaver," I tell my big brother as I give him an appreciative hug. "You too, Braxton. I didn't think you and Sophie could make it," I say as I hug him as well.

"I dropped Sophie, Lily Claire, and Vivian over at Myer's place with Dallas and the kids. They are going to spend the evening making Christmas cookies with Beau. She needed out of the house, and I needed some mother-in-law-free time, so she talked me into coming with Myer. She's sorry she couldn't make it."

"Well, I'm glad to have you both here, and I know Brandt will be too. I completely understand why the new mommies aren't able. There will always be next year, if you two studs don't ruin it again," I assure him.

"I make no promises," Myer chimes up.

Braxton chuckles.

"Anything else you need help with before this thing gets underway, sis?"

I look around. Everything looks ready.

"I don't think so. Grab yourselves a beer and go outside and find Brandt. People should start coming in the next hour or so."

They do just that as the bartender and the servers arrive. I show Pete to the den, and Dottie goes over the food instructions with the girls. Then, she and Marvin head home.

The band gets set up and begins to play as guests start arriving.

Elle and Walker are the next ones to show, and before long, the house is humming with laughter and conversation.

Everyone seems to be enjoying the cocktails and food. People are dancing, and I finally relax and soak up the joy of being in my new home with my love and our people.

It's pure bliss.

Eight

BRANDT

"THE PLACE TURNED OUT GOOD," BRAXTON PRAISES AS he takes in the glass sunroom I added off the veranda for Bellamy.

"It did, and it feels good, knowing that most of it was done with my own two hands. With lots of help from all your hands too, that is. Thank you, if I didn't say it enough at the time," I say as I look at the group of Myer, Walker, and Braxton.

Walker slaps me on the back. "You're welcome, Doc. Besides, you're about to get the chance to pay it forward. I wanted to talk to you all. I need help with a surprise for Elle," he begins.

"We're all ears," Braxton offers.

"You know that chapel where your parents got married? Elle has her heart set on us having our wedding there, too, but the church moved a few years back and let that little chapel fall into ruin. The land it stands on is going to be turned into a neighborhood park, but the pastor of the church, who owns it, agreed to let us donate our time to do the repairs, so we can use it for our ceremony. Afterward, it will serve as an event space and restroom facility for the park."

"What kind of repairs are we talking about?" Myer asks him.

"Nothing major. Painting, laying a new floor where they tore out the pews, fixing a roof leak and maybe a few plumbing issues. I also said we'd bring some tractors out and clear some of the land for the playground equipment when the time comes," he gives us the list as he pleads with his eyes.

"Count me in," Braxton agrees.

"Yeah, me too." Myer is next to jump in.

"Make that three. I'll be happy to help," I tell him.

"Thanks, guys. It's going to mean a lot to Elle. Can you keep it under your hats though? The pastor gave me a key, and I'm going to sneak over there Christmas Eve and string the place with twinkling lights and fill it with flowers, so I can take my girl there Christmas morning and tell her the good news. He was the one who married your parents, Brax. He remembers them fondly, and he agreed to be a part of our wedding," he says.

The tremble in Braxton's jaw as he reaches out and clinches Walker's shoulder says all he needs to. It obviously means a lot to him as well.

"Since we're on the subject, I'm working on my own Christmas surprise for Dallas. I'm fixing up my uncle's old carriage and turning it into a working sleigh. I want to extend the cab and add upholstered benches that face each other. Foster and Truett built a hitch that will hold four horses to attach to the front. I'm hoping if we get another good snow before Christmas Eve, I can have it ready and take her and the kids for a sleigh ride through the woods to Mom and Pop's house. We can keep it and store it, and as our families grow and all our kids get older, we can pull it out each year," he says.

"We could add retractable wheels so that it can be used as a sleigh or buggy. That way, even if it doesn't snow, you can use it," Walker suggests.

"And Doreen found these cool, large bronze bells at the antique store. She's been trying to figure out what to do with them. They'd make great sleigh bells," Braxton suggests.

"I'm available the next few nights once the clinic closes," I add.

He nods. "Sophie wants a hot tub. Which means I need to do a reinforced add-on to the current deck. She also wants a tin roof over it, so she can soak in it when it rains and enjoy the sound of it hitting the tin," Braxton starts.

"We're in," we all say before he even asks.

"Thanks, guys," he offers.

"Well, Doc, what about you? You need help with something for Bells for Christmas?"

"Nope. I bought her diamond earrings," I say.

"Smart man," Walker praises.

"I will take a rain check on the help though. She wants the garden out back restored to its former glory with a working fountain and gazebo. She wants to have our wedding out there."

"When are you thinking?" Myer asks.

"Next spring will be the best time to work on it. We aren't planning to marry until she's done with school in Denver, so it won't be for another couple of years. So, it's not a rush."

"You just tell us when you're ready to get on it, Doc," Walker says.

I nod. It's nice to be a part of a brotherhood of sorts. These guys aren't just friends; they treat one another like family. I didn't have that before I moved from Portland to Poplar Falls. I didn't even know it existed.

"Hey, what are y'all doing out here, looking so serious?" Elle asks.

"None of your business, woman. If you girls can have your secret talks, so can we," Walker tells her.

"Are you 'bout done? I want to dance, and if you don't come to swing me around this dance floor, I'm going to be forced to let one of Bells's handsome cousins do it," she dares.

"Gotta go, fellas," he says before he takes the last drink from his bottle and sets it on the railing.

"Whipped," Braxton yells after him, and Walker's middle fingers wave at us from behind his back as he follows after Elle.

"I think that's my cue to go find Bells as well. She's been flitting around, making sure everyone else is enjoying themselves. I want to make sure she is doing the same," I tell Braxton and Myer.

"Go find your girl, Doc. We're going to hang out a while longer until Sophie calls and lets me know that she and her mother are ready to go back home. We'll catch up to you before we head out."

I find her leaning against the back of the house, wineglass in hand.

The sight of her lit by the moonlight, watching guests dance as the band plays, takes my breath away.

I walk over and offer her my hand.

She looks up and smiles. "I thought you weren't much of a dancer."

I shrug. "It's growing on me," I tell her as she sets her glass aside and takes my hand.

I guide her out into the crowd and pull her close.

"The party turned out amazing. Just like you," I praise her.

"Yeah, it did. Thank you for indulging me."

I plan to spend the rest of my life indulging her.

Nine

SONIA

THE PARTY IS BEGINNING TO DWINDLE. WE ARE ALL A LITTLE tired and a lot wobbly on our feet. I take a break from the dance floor and walk to the front porch to get some fresh air.

The cold winter air hits my damp skin and instantly cools me down. Bellamy had large propane heaters brought in to line the porch and back deck, so I move closer to the one on my left and place my hands on the railing. It's a beautiful night. The stars are so bright. The music drifts out through the window, and I close my eyes and soak up the Christmas cheer.

I wait as a few guests meander out and to their cars. When a light breeze kicks up, I turn to go back in when I hear my name being called.

I look out over the yard, and I search the darkness.

Finally, a figure steps out of the shadows and into the light.

Ricky.

I look around to see if anyone else is out there.

"What are you doing here?" I ask as my eyes come back to him.

"I wanted to talk to you. I figured you'd be at this shindig."

"I don't think you're welcome. You shouldn't have come here."

"I know. I won't stay. I just wanted to see you and wish you a merry Christmas. I miss you," he says, and my stupid, traitorous heart skips a beat.

He takes a few tentative steps forward, and I back up. He stops, puts his hands in his pockets, and lowers his head.

"I wanted to apologize. I was angry, and I didn't mean all those things I said at Doreen's party."

He looks up, no doubt waiting for my reaction. I just stay quiet, so he continues, "I'm a mess, but I'm getting on my feet. I want to be a good husband. I want to take care of you and buy you that house. I want to make babies with you and be a family. I'd be a good dad. I know I would. I just need you to believe in me again. To believe in us."

He is saying all the things I wanted to hear two months ago. All of the things that I convinced myself he could be.

"Say something," he pleads.

"I don't know what to say," I whisper.

"Say you'll give me a chance, give our marriage a second chance. We should be spending tomorrow night together. It'll be our first Christmas. Aren't you always preaching about forgiveness? All I'm asking is that you grant it to me, your husband."

"I do forgive you, Ricky."

He smiles at that and starts forward, but I put my hand up to stop him.

"You're saying all the right stuff. Everything that you promised me when I agreed to be your wife, and you still have the potential to be all that. But the problem is, I fell in love with who you could be and not who you are. I gave you all of me, the real me, but you never gave me the real you. I needed you to *be that man*, not have the potential to be him," I confess.

He drops his head. "You've let those girls get into your head and turn you against me. Now, nothing I say or do is going to make a difference, is it?"

"This isn't anyone's fault, except for yours and mine. I was content, having part of you, and you were content with letting me. I've seen what real love looks like and what we had doesn't compare. I want something real. I deserve it."

"Right," he bites out.

Before he can continue, the front door opens, and a giggling Elle stumbles out with Walker close behind, guiding her.

"Whoa, what are you doing out here by yourself?" she asks when she sees me.

"You have got to be fucking kidding me," Walker hisses.

Elle looks up at him in confusion. "What?" she asks.

"If it isn't my best friend, Walker Reid." Ricky pokes at the hornet.

"Braxton," Walker yells.

The door opens, and Braxton walks out, followed by Brandt.

"You bellowed," Braxton deadpans before his gaze follows Walker's, and he grimaces.

"Here, get Elle for me, will you?" Walker says as he hands her off to her brother without taking his eyes off Ricky.

He doesn't get a chance to move beyond that because, in the blink of an eye, Brandt is off the porch and has Ricky by the collar.

"You got a lot of nerve, showing up at my house. Bellamy still has a scar on her arm from your teeth marks," he spits in Ricky's face.

Ricky very unwisely grins at him and says, "Good."

That's when Brandt tears back and punches him so hard that his head flies around, and blood splatters all over the front of Brandt's shirt.

Elle screams, and that causes everyone left from the party to come flooding out onto the porch.

Ricky stumbles backward, and he gets up and rushes at Brandt.

"Ricky, stop," I scream.

"He fucking hit me, Sonia!"

"Brandt, don't; he's not worth it," Braxton says as he lets Elle go and hops off the porch. He locks his arms around Brandt's chest and forces him backward.

"Get out of my yard, and don't you step foot here, the clinic, or anywhere near Bellamy again," Brandt warns.

Ricky brings his eyes to mine as he holds his nose. Then, he looks back at Brandt. "Fuck, I'm sorry. I didn't mean that. I was drunk that night. I'd never hurt a woman in my right mind," Ricky tries to explain.

Braxton is the one to answer him, "The drunk excuse doesn't cut it, man. We've all been shit-faced before. Hell, we've all been pissed off and shit-faced before, but even in that state, we'd never, ever lay a hand on a woman. An apology is good and all, but if you want to earn any of our respect or, hell, even your own respect, then you need help. Counseling, AA, anger management … something."

"Would any of that make a difference?" Ricky directs his question to me.

"Not to me, but it would to the future woman in your life," I tell him, and pain slices through me as I see the acceptance sink in.

He starts walking backward, and without another word, he turns and struts out of sight.

Elle is by my side in an instant. "Are you all right?" she asks.

I nod. "I'm fine," I tell her.

She wraps her arms around me anyway and holds on to me. "Do you want to come and have a sleepover with me tonight?"

"Bells has already claimed me for the night."

"That sneaky bitch," she grumbles.

"I'll see you at the festival tomorrow night. You're helping Mom and me at her wreath booth, remember?"

"I'll be there," she assures me.

"What did I miss?"

We turn to see Bells in the doorway, staring at the blood on Brandt's shirt.

"Walker got mouthy, and I had to teach him a lesson." He shrugs.

"Hey, why couldn't it have been Braxton?" Walker complains.

"Like she'd buy that," Braxton retorts.

Walker looks at him. "I'll have you know that you are indeed the bigger asshole of the two of us. Right, baby?" he calls to Elle.

"Maybe, but you are definitely the mouthiest."

"That's it; no lovin' for you tonight," he threatens.

"That's fine. I'm staying the night here with Sonia anyway," Elle retorts.

"You are?" I ask.

"Yeah, Walker has to get up early for work, and we haven't had a sleepover in a while," she says and then turns to Bells. "You can loan me something to sleep in, right?"

"Of course," Bells answers.

"See what you did?" Walker says to Braxton.

"I can't help she'd rather stay here than at your house."

"She loves my house. Tell him, Elle. It's like staying at a five-star hotel," Walker prompts.

"Yep. A five-star hotel with so-so room service," she agrees.

"That's the last time you get served deer jerky breakfast in bed, woman!" He feigns being hurt.

"Come on; it's getting cold out here. Let's go in and put some warm PJs on," Bells beckons.

We get snuggled into bed with a bowl of popcorn to watch *The Santa Clause* while Brandt sees the last of the guests out and locks up.

"Are you sure you're okay?" Bells asks me.

"I am. It's weird, but I think I needed to hear his apology to let go. It gave me some kind of closure or something," I admit.

"Good. Now, you're free to find your happily ever after," Bells declares.

"I don't know about that, but I do feel a little freer."

"Do you guys remember when we were in high school, and Dusty Owensby broke up with me? I was so devastated and swore I'd never love anyone as much as I loved him. I thought my heart couldn't possibly recover," Elle says.

We nod. *How could we forget?*

"Do you remember what Gram told us? That God had our husbands caught in a bush somewhere and that we shouldn't be worried when someone broke our hearts, but thankful because that person had been in our way."

"Yeah, vaguely. I remember us thinking she was bananas, talking about that bush," I answer.

"She said Abraham was told to take his son, Isaac, up on Mount Moriah and offer him as a sacrifice. He was confused about why God would ask this of him when he promised him this son, but he was obedient even though he didn't understand. At the last moment before he brought the knife down, God stopped him. He had a goat trapped in a bush for the sacrifice. He just wanted to know Abraham trusted him. Then, she said that we should trust if a boy walks out of our life, then he wasn't the one. That God had our husband trapped in a bush somewhere, so we should just live our lives, find ourselves, and when the time was right, God would set him loose for us."

"Do you believe it's true?" I ask her.

"I didn't until he set Walker loose on me. Walker Reid—who would have guessed that?"

"Isn't that the truth?" Bellamy adds.

"He had Brandt trapped in a bush while I was wasting time with Derrick."

"Well, if he has mine trapped somewhere, maybe he'll finally set him loose now that Ricky is out of the way. Too bad I had to marry him before I realized he wasn't the one. Ugh, I'm going to be a twenty-four-year-old divorcée. Gross."

"Maybe it's not you who isn't ready. Maybe he has to get the one he picked out for you sorted before he's ready to be set loose. That was the case with Walker," Elle ponders.

That's a good point.

"Hmm, you might be right. I guess I'll just live my life and let it work itself out."

"That's my girl," Bells says.

We hear a throat clear, and our eyes move to the door. Brandt is standing there, grinning at us.

"You girls look comfy. I guess this means I'm on my own tonight, huh?" he asks Bells.

"Looks like it unless I make it to the end of the movie, still awake. I might sneak in with you, but don't wait up because I make no promises," she says before popping a piece of popcorn in her mouth and pressing play on the remote.

I lay my head on her shoulder.

"You girls enjoy your night. And just shout if you need anything."

"Another bottle of wine would be great," Bells says.

"Red or white?"

"Red," she and I both say.

"Coming right up," he says before walking off.

"Yep, totally worth the wait," I say.

Ten

CHARLOTTE

"WE HAVE THIS DESIGN THAT WE HAVEN'T launched yet; we could do it exclusively for you," I say.

The drop-dead gorgeous woman across from me inspects the ring. She picks it up, turns it, and holds it up to the light. Then, she tries it on.

Valentina Demperio is one of our select clients. She's a woman who knows what she wants, and she will get just that. She spends a lot of money on her jewelry collection and is a fan of giving generous gifts to her friends, family, and staff. She fell in love with Sophie's designs last year, and she is a frequent high-end shopper with us. Anything she buys has to be one of a kind and never replicated. Sophie even designs to her specifications at her requests from time to time.

"I'll take it. I want the sapphire replaced with an emerald though. I'd also like the wrap bracelet. One in white gold and two in yellow gold. Both fourteen karat. When will the ruby necklace for my mother be ready?"

I look down at my tablet. "The necklace will be ready next week. I can have the sapphire replaced, and the ring and bracelets can be ready to be picked up with the necklace, if that works for you?"

"Yes, that's fine. Can you do a matching necklace for me? Just a tad bit less ostentatious than Mother's. We'll be wearing them with our gowns for the Christmas Ball this year. Oh, and add diamond hair combs too. No stones, just the diamonds. Headbands are too over the top. I want to wear something more elegant this year."

"You got it. I can email over the designs for approval as soon as Sophie sends them, and we'll make sure to have them ready in time as well."

I'm going to have to visit the warehouse myself to have them bump this order ahead of all the other holiday orders. I don't know Valentina all that well, but I know well enough to be cautious, and the very last thing you want to do is piss off a Demperio.

"That will be fantastic. I'll have the money transferred as soon as I receive your invoice. Oh, by the way, do you guys do engagement rings?" she asks.

I look up to her and smile. "We certainly can. Are congratulations in order?"

"Not yet, but very soon. I'll give my boyfriend your card. You know me so well. I'm sure you can help him design something perfect for me. Something at least seven carats," she says.

"We can absolutely guide him in the right direction," I agree.

"Thank you, Charlotte," she says as she stands.

The bell chimes above the café door, and her eyes cut to the front.

"Speak of the devil, here comes my love now," she says as an insanely beautiful man walks to us.

"Charlotte, I'd like you to meet my boyfriend, Nicco Mastreoni, Nicco, this is my private jeweler, Charlotte Claiborne."

"It's lovely to meet you, Charlotte," he says as he places a hand on the small of Valentina's back.

"Likewise," I greet.

As he turns to speak to her, I mouth to her, *Congratulations*, as I fan myself.

She winks at me.

"Are you ready to go, sweetheart?" he asks.

"Yes, we were just finishing up. Thank you again, Charlotte. I will be on the lookout for your email."

With that, they walk out hand in hand. *Whew, she's a lucky duck.*

I gather my things, pay the tab, and hurry back to the office. This little impromptu meeting took longer than I'd expected, and I have to get back for my three o'clock appointment.

"Thank you again for coming in. We look forward to seeing your new marketing ideas at the first of the year."

I lead the executives from the new firm Sophia Doreen Designs signed with from the conference room to the elevator.

"It was our pleasure," the tall, dark, and handsome one says with a wink as the doors open, and they step inside.

What a flirt.

I give him a little wave as the doors close and then head back to my office to grab my purse and call it a day.

"Charlotte, you have a call on line two," my assistant, Sara, says as I pass her desk.

"Thanks. I'll grab it at my desk. You can go ahead and head home. I'll lock up."

"Perfect. I can make it to the deli before they close. Have a great weekend," she calls after me as she closes her laptop and packs it in her tote.

When I make it to my office, I kick off my heels and slide

into my chair. It's been a crazy week with holiday sales, and I am exhausted.

I press the blinking light on the phone and settle back.

"Sophia Doreen Designs. Talk to me," I say with fake enthusiasm.

"Hi, gorgeous."

"I'm sorry, but I didn't catch your name," I say as a smile creeps into my brain fog.

"It's your favorite addiction," he drawls.

"Hmm, not ringing a bell. You'll have to be more specific," I tease.

"Oh, I can be more specific, sweetheart. Are you alone?"

I giggle.

"Shit, slow down, man. We aren't in a race," he says.

"I don't get it. Are we role-playing?" I ask.

"I'm sorry, what?" he asks.

"I thought you were revving me up for phone sex?"

"Whoa, that was close. Stay in your lane," he yells.

I hear muffled swearing and a symphony of loud blasts.

"Payne, where are you?" I ask.

"I'm in a death trap. That's where I am," he bites out.

An offended voice in the background curses him, and he chuckles.

"Payne Henderson, where are you?" I ask as suspicion and hope begin to bubble.

"I'm in the back of a taxi, on my way from JFK into Manhattan, watching my life flash before my eyes. Seriously, why do any of you bother to honk your horn when everyone is laying on them all at once? That's not how they work."

I jump to my feet. "You're here. In New York City?"

"Yes, ma'am. I decided to surprise my favorite girl for Christmas."

I scream.

"Damn, I hope that was a good screech and not a *what the fuck were you thinking, coming here* screech."

"Oh my God, I can't believe you got on a plane. Where are you? Or where are you headed?"

"Sophie gave me your address," he answers.

"Oh no, hand your driver the phone," I demand.

"I don't think he needs the distraction."

"Oh, please, New York taxi drivers can drive with their eyes closed. Give him the phone," I insist.

"Hello?" an unfamiliar voice comes over the line.

"Hey, reroute. You bring that sexy cowboy straight to my office at the corner of Thirty-Sixth and Park."

I hear more cursing before Payne's voice comes back on.

"I'll be there in twenty."

"I'll be waiting," I say before clicking off the line.

I pick up the receiver and dial Sophie's number.

"You're welcome," Sophie says instead of a greeting.

"You sneaky bitch. I can't believe you didn't warn me!"

"He wanted to surprise you. I told him you were bummed that you weren't going to be able to come to Colorado before the holidays to meet Lily Claire and see us all. I obviously can't travel right now, so he asked me to help him. I got him on a flight and helped him navigate JFK and the taxi lines."

"Well, I'm surprised. He is on his way to the office now. I've got to go. I need to spruce up, go splash water on my bits, and spritz on some perfume or something."

"It's Payne, remember? The guy you went camping with, rode four-wheelers in the mud with, and stayed out all night long, dancing and drinking with. He knows what all your bits smell like," she says with amusement.

"It's been months since he got a load of my bits, and I want them in tip-top shape when he sees them again. Now, bye. I'll call you tomorrow," I say before hanging up, and I can hear her laughter before I click off the line.

I run to my private bathroom and do the best I can. I'm just swiping on my lip gloss when I hear the ring. I run to my desk and see the doorman is calling up.

I hit the speaker. "Yes?"

"Miss Claiborne, there is a Payne Henderson here to see you. I've explained that it is after hours, and I can't just let him into the building, but he is a bit impatient."

"That's okay, Barry. He's a friend of mine. You can let him up."

"Yes, ma'am. Right away."

He hangs up, and my stomach fills with anticipation.

Five minutes later, the elevator doors open, and Payne steps into our front foyer, looking like a country dream. I don't say a word; I just take off running for him. He drops his duffel bag and catches me just as I fling myself into his arms and crush my mouth to his.

His hands slide from my waist and settle on the curve of my ass before he hoists me up and starts carrying me forward. I continue to assault his mouth as we pass my secretary's desk. When he makes it to the opening of the hallway, he stops.

I break from his lips long enough to say, "The last door on the right."

He hurries us to the door of my office, and I reach behind me and frantically feel for the handle. I finally find it, and we lurch forward as I twist, bursting into the space.

He carries me to my desk and sets me on the edge. I pull back and tug his shirttail from the waistband of his jeans and start unbuttoning them. My fingers can't move fast enough. Once I get to the top, he shrugs it off his shoulders and leans back to pull his white T-shirt off before dropping it on the floor.

I rake my nails through his smattering of dark chest hair and down his rippled abs to the button of his jeans and pop it open. I'm too impatient to wait for him to slide them down, so my hand fishes into the front until I find what I'm looking for. Hard and ready. I wrap my fingers around him and tug gently, and he groans.

"I have always wanted to have office sex," I confess.

"Happy to oblige, ma'am."

That accent and those polite words of his turn me on so much.

"I've been wet since you called me. I thought you'd never get here," I tell him as I slide my hand as far as I can and back up.

"Yeah, well, I've been on an airplane for three hours, unsuccessfully trying to hide a painful erection from a very attentive flight attendant," he grits out.

"She'd better not have been the one who got you hard, cowboy," I say as I squeeze him tight.

He moans out, "No, ma'am."

His hands are rubbing circles on the tops of my thighs, and he slowly moves them up to bring the hem of my skirt with them. I bear up, so he can slide it to my waist. Then, he takes the back of his hand and runs his knuckles over the front of my black lace panties, and my legs start to shake as he grazes my clit. He grins at my reaction and then slides a finger under the lace and glides it through my wetness before pumping it inside of me.

"Oh, yes," I cry as I remove my hand from him and bring my arms back to brace myself against the cool wood of my desk.

I close my eyes and throw my head back as he adds another finger and starts a delicious swirl. He plays for just a few moments before he loses his patience and withdraws, ripping my panties down my legs. I open my eyes just as he drops his jeans to the floor and steps out of them before he grabs my hips and yanks me forward. I let out a surprised yelp and then watch as he spreads my legs wide to give himself better access. Then, he reaches back for the chair that is in front of my desk and pulls it closer, so he can sit before me. His fingers find their way back to my opening. He uses his finger and thumb to work me up into a frenzy, and then he brings his mouth to my center and starts to lap at me wildly.

"Oh, that's it, cowboy. Right there," I manage to breathe out as I grab his hair and hold on.

He sucks my clit between his teeth and bites down lightly, and I buck off the desk.

That's when he slides the chair back and away from me.

I voice my protest, and he stands and lifts me off the desk and onto my feet.

He turns me, bends me over the desk, and hikes my skirt back up. He palms the cheek, and then he gives it a quick slap before he leans over me and says into my ear, "Have you been naughty or nice this year, Miss Claiborne?"

"Naughty. Very, very naughty," I answer.

He gives me another quick smack, and I moan.

"Are you going to be nice the rest of the year?" he asks.

"Probably not."

That gets me another lick, and I can feel the heat radiating off my skin. He soothingly caresses his hand over the spot just before he plants a gentle kiss there.

Then, he takes his knee and spreads my legs before he bends back to my ear. I am all sensation. I feel his heat and the rise and fall of his chest against my back and the slick finish of the desk against my tight nipples. The sound of our heavy breaths mingles with the sound of the city outside the window.

He sucks my earlobe into his mouth, and his teeth sink in.

A shiver runs down my spine.

"You like that?" he asks.

"Stop teasing me, Payne. I need you inside of me now," I demand.

"Are you sure you're ready?" he asks as he slides his hand between my legs again. "Oh, yes, you're dripping," he tells me what I already know.

"Payne, I swear if you don't—"

My retort dies on my lips as he thrusts into me from behind.

Finally.

I bear up to give him plenty of access, and he takes the opportunity to bring his hands around, removing my blouse. Then, he undoes the front clasp of my bra with expert ease, and it falls to the sides. He cups my breasts as he pumps into me, and his thumbs circle my aching nipples.

The air kicks on, and the vent above us blows across our sweat-slicked skin. Gooseflesh crawls up my back and intensifies the mounting wave of pleasure that is bubbling to the surface.

I start to push up onto the toe of my heels to meet his movement and rock into him. I can feel the warmth spreading down my spine to my core. Payne releases one of my breasts, and his thumb finds my clit. He presses into me with the perfect pressure my body needs to let go, and I slam my hands against the top of the desk, sending papers flying as my legs quake from the orgasm shooting through me. I grab hold of the object beside me and hurl it across the room as I cry out.

"Yes, Payne. Yes, yes, yes," I chant as the euphoria rushes over my limbs and I melt into the wood.

He continues to pump in and out until his knees buckle, and he releases into me on a groan. Spent, he falls against my back, and we just lie there until our heart rates come down. Then, he kisses my neck and stands.

I get to my feet, a little shaky on my heels, and turn to face him.

He wraps me in his arms and kisses me gently.

"Hi, gorgeous. It's good to see you," he says.

I lace my arms around his neck. "Really? I couldn't tell."

He growls and starts to back me up until my thighs hit the desk again.

"I'm teasing. I'm teasing. You have thoroughly worn me out, and now, I'm ravenous. Feed me before I get cranky," I demand.

"Woman, I just made you come so hard, you threw a stapler and knocked a plant over, and you are threatening to get cranky?"

I stand and smooth my skirt back over my hips and clasp my bra. "Yep."

"Damn, I missed you," he says as he reaches for his tee.

We get dressed, and I call my car service to come pick us up. I order takeout delivery from my favorite Chinese restaurant on the way. I have a feeling we will be staying in tonight.

Eleven

PAYNE

I STIR AT THE CLANG OF POUNDING THAT SOUNDS LIKE A JACKHAMMER trying to bust its way through the wall to Charlotte's bedroom. I feel her body jolt, and I know it woke her up too.

"What the fuck is that?" I ask without opening my eyes.

She rolls into my side and throws her arm across my waist. "They are doing construction on the building beside this one, and they start with that racket every single morning at seven a.m. on the dot," she huffs.

"Every morning? Shit, for how long?"

"Six months now. They were supposed to be finished by the end of November but no such luck. It's not that big a deal during the week because I'm usually up and gone by this time."

I open one eye and look at her. "You go into the office earlier than seven a.m.?"

That surprises me. When she's in Poplar Falls, the woman never gets out of bed until I forcibly make her get up.

"No, I go to my SoulCycle class at six, but when I'm off, I usually wait until the eight a.m. class," she answers.

"What the hell is SoulCycle?"

"It's a class where we ride stationary bikes and follow the instructions of a military-type tyrant who tries to kill us before the end of the hour. It's fun. You want to try it? I can bring one visitor per session."

"You want me to get on a bike and pretend I'm riding it, but it doesn't move?"

"Well, yes. It's good exercise, and there's a screen on each bike that shows you riding through a trail or on a beach."

I just stare at her like she's grown a second head.

"How about we just get a couple of bikes from that thingy outside that has them all piled on it and actually ride them through that big, beautiful park you keep telling me about?" I suggest.

She wrinkles her nose. "I pay a lot for those classes, so I can eat anything I want, and my backside stays firm."

I tilt my head as I tug the sheet that's covering her down to the tops of her thighs, and glance at the perfect curve of her.

"I like your ass exactly the way it is, and I can think of much more fun ways to keep it nice and toned," I say as I scoop her up and pull her on top of me.

She lays her chin on my chest and raises an eyebrow at me. "Okay, cowboy, you win this round. No class, but don't think you're getting out of dinner with my friends tonight. No amount of distraction sex is getting me to cancel. They have been dying to see what keeps me hopping on planes and flying to the middle of nowhere, and I'm going to show you off."

"I'll make a deal with you. You get me out of this loud construction zone and spend the afternoon showing me what it is you love about this noisy, crowded city, and I'll be happy to let you parade me around in front of your friends tonight."

"Deal. By the way, how long are you staying?"

"Until Christmas night. I have an overnight flight back to Denver."

"That means you'll be coming to my parents' house for

Christmas. I can't wait for my mother to get a gander at you. You think Vivian Marshall is a handful? My mother taught her everything she knows."

I wrap my arms around her and pull her up until we're nose to nose. "I can handle your momma," I tell her before I take her mouth, and then I lie back and block out the commotion outside while she uses that mouth on me.

We spend the afternoon in the elbow-to-elbow crowds. Everyone's in a hurry to get somewhere, and no one cares if they are in your space. I try to give her my full attention as she exuberantly spills the history of every sight. I might not enjoy all the walking, all the noise, or all the rude people, but I love every second of watching her excitedly act as my personal tour guide through New York from river to river. The food isn't bad either. We eat our way across the city, and I have to admit, the bagels and pizza are both superior to the ones you can get in Colorado.

"I told you. Nothing compares to a slice of pie in the city," she says as we turn down yet another corner. "We're here," she screeches as she turns to face me and takes my hand, pulling me into a crowded square.

What has to be thousands of people are bunched into the courtyard between two buildings. I'm starting to feel claustrophobic when she stops and points up. I follow her gaze up to an enormous Christmas tree covered in lights. It's as tall as a building.

"Ta-da! The Rockefeller Center Christmas Tree," she says as she stares up at the twinkling branches. "Isn't it a breathtaking sight?" she asks.

I keep my eyes firmly on the woman in front of me as I answer, "It sure is."

Just then, a large man looking down at his phone plows into us. He looks up as if just realizing he is walking and steps around us.

"You're excused, asshole," I yell after him.

Charlotte grabs my face with her hands. "You've had enough, haven't you?"

"I'm fine," I tell her.

"Come on, cowboy. Let's get you somewhere less congested before you blow a gasket."

She fists my shirt and drags me through the spiderweb of limbs and down another street that looks the same as all the others.

Then, she darts into a side door leading into a hotel and walks us through the lobby, toward the back, and to what looks to be the entrance to a restaurant.

We stop at the hostess.

"Hi, Brit. Are the others here?" she asks the woman standing behind the podium.

"Hi, Miss Claiborne. Yes, your party arrived a few minutes ago. They're waiting at the bar until we get your regular table ready."

"Thank you," she says as she grabs my hand and leads me past the lady and into a dimly lit lounge with small tables and a large mahogany bar.

My ears and my head appreciate the quiet as we walk to join a small crowd standing at a table to the left of the bar.

"Charlotte!" one of the girls calls as we approach. "I already ordered you a white wine spritzer, you tardy bitch."

"Thanks, hon," she says as we make it to her friend, and they air-kiss each other's cheeks.

"Wow, who's your friend?" the girl asks as she looks around Charlotte to me.

"This is my Colorado mountain man I've been telling you about, Payne Henderson. This is Cora McDaniels. She's one of my oldest friends. We went to college together," Charlotte introduces.

The girl sticks her hand out to me, palm down. I look at her hand, and not knowing what she's looking for, I clutch her fingers and shake.

She and Charlotte both chuckle as I release her.

A waitress in a black tie comes over with a tray and hands Charlotte a wineglass.

"Can I get you anything, sir?" she asks me.

"What do you have on tap?"

"Tap?" she repeats back to me, clearly confused.

"Yeah, beer. Draft beer?"

"Oh." She recovers. "We have several craft beers available. Let me grab you a beer menu. I'll be right back."

With that, she sashays off to the bar.

"A beer menu?" I ask Charlotte.

Before she can say anything, a pompous voice from behind answers, "Sorry, they don't serve Bud Light here."

I turn to see a dark-haired guy in a navy suit. He offers me his hand, and I just look at it.

He clears his throat and puts it in his pocket.

"I suggest the Kentucky Vanilla Barrel Ale," he offers as he brings his glass of amber liquid to his lips.

The waitress returns with the card in hand.

I wave it off. "Just bring me a Maker's Mark, straight up."

"Right away, sir."

"And drop the sir. The name's Payne," I tell her.

She blushes as she repeats my name, "Payne. Got it. Coming right up."

She rushes off again, and Charlotte narrows her eyes at me.

"You can't just start throwing all that cowboy hotness around and springing it on unsuspecting New York women. These females are not prepared. It's unfair."

"You're a nut," I say as I pull her into me.

"Charlotte, my mother wanted me to ask if you had received your Christmas Eve invitation yet? She hasn't gotten your RSVP," another gray suit asks her.

"Oh, I must have forgotten," she says and then looks up at me. "Did you bring anything other than jeans?"

"Nope."

"Hmm," she says, assessing me. "You wouldn't want to go to a charity party with me, would you?"

I shake my head.

"Tyler, tell your mother I'm not going to be able to make it this year. I have company from out of town."

"Your mother is not going to be happy," Cora says, and she turns to her.

"My mother won't care if I miss one year," Charlotte disagrees.

"If you say so. You want another?" she asks as she dangles her empty glass.

"Of course," Charlotte says as she downs the last drop from her glass.

The waitress makes it back with my drink and hurries back off for two more drinks for the girls. A third female joins them, and they start gabbing about some new boutique opening.

"So, what do you do, Payne?" Suit Number One asks.

I cut my eyes to him. "I'm sorry, but I didn't catch your name."

"Blake Thornton, and this is my associate Tyler McMann," the navy suit introduces me to his pal.

"Associate. Is that what you call your friends in New York?" I ask.

"No, we're business partners," he clarifies.

"So, not friends?"

"Yes, friends as well."

Why didn't he just say that?

"I'm a farmer," I tell them, and the expression on their faces is confusion.

"A farmer? As in plowing fields and growing things like vegetables?"

"Yeah, something like that."

"That's ... interesting," Blake says for lack of a better response.

"It can be," I say as I gulp the rest of my drink and signal for the waitress to bring me another.

She nods at me, and I focus back on the associates.

"We are traders," he tells me.

"Traders?"

"Yes, on Wall Street. We buy and sell stocks for our clients," he explains.

"Sounds fascinating," I remark.

"Quite. I bet doing farm things is as well," Tyler adds.

"Yep."

We stand there in awkward silence as the girls talk nonstop.

Charlotte pulls another girl away and walks her to me.

"Payne, this is Mila; she's my baby sister. She's having drinks with us but not dinner. She's a model, so she only eats when it's absolutely necessary," she introduces.

"You're such a bitch," Mila says before she turns to me. "It's nice to meet you, Payne," she says.

"Same."

"Damn, that accent is sexy. I bet my sister chains you to the bed and just makes you talk to her all night."

"What, and waste all this?" Charlotte says as she gestures wildly at me from head to foot.

"Yeah, I see your point."

Charlotte turns and holds out her third empty glass to me.

"You'd better slow down. I'll not have you passing out on me tonight," I whisper into her hair.

Blake stares a hole past Tyler at us, and if looks could ignite, I would be bursting into a fireball. Mr. Navy Suit obviously has a hard-on for Charlotte. Sucks to be him.

"Not gonna happen," she says to me, oblivious to his attention.

"How long have we been waiting? I'm going to go ask Brit how much longer before we're seated," Cora announces before walking off.

"I'll come with you. I need to powder my nose," Charlotte calls after her. "I'll be right back," she tells me as I take the glass from her hand.

I watch as she walks out of sight, and every man in the bar trains his eyes to focus on her backside in that figure-hugging dress.

"Stunning, isn't she?" Blake asks as he, too, watches her go.

I cut my eyes to him and do not react to his question. "Another round, fellas?" I offer instead.

"Sure," Tyler says, and I don't wait for Blake to answer before I make my way to the bar.

I'm chatting with the bartender when Charlotte and Cora return. She doesn't see me as they pass and continues to the guys. I pick up the three glasses in front of me and follow them. When I make it to the group, I hear Charlotte's angry voice.

"What did you just say?"

The guys turn around and face Charlotte. She has her arms crossed on her chest, and she's scowling at them.

"Charlotte, did you find out how much longer the table will be?" Tyler deflects.

"I asked you a question."

Blake clears his throat. "We were discussing work."

"Liar. I heard you talking shit."

He looks around nervously. He's obviously met drunk, pissed-off Charlotte before. "Charlotte, let's not make a scene."

"A scene? Oh, I haven't begun to make a scene yet. Why don't you repeat what you just said to Tyler?"

"Char, calm down."

I can see this is about to be bad, so I interrupt.

"Fellas, your drinks," I say and hand off the glasses I'm holding.

"Thank you," Tyler says as he takes his.

"When did you become such a snob, Blake?" Charlotte continues.

That clearly rubs him the wrong way because he loses the fake facade and his expression turns icy.

"Snob? That's rich, Charlotte. You and I come from the same breed."

"What does that mean?"

"Look, if you want to go slumming with the farmer, that's fine and dandy, but that doesn't mean I have to pretend to like it," he spits out.

"Did you just hear what came out of your mouth? Do you think that because he's a farmer, you're somehow superior to him?"

"Charlotte, please," he asks as if it was a silly question.

I step up to intervene, and she throws her arm out to halt me.

"This farmer has his own four-hundred-acre orchard. He owns and runs it like a well-oiled machine. He lives in a house that he built with his own two hands. Do you even know how to use a hammer? He drives a John Deere, a big-ass truck, and a speed boat. He can ride a horse and a bull. You have to pay someone to take you around the city because you don't even have a license."

She leans in close. "Want to know what else he can ride really well that you never will? Me."

I come up and wrap an arm around her waist. "All right, down, tiger."

She shrugs me off and gets in his face. "That farmer is more of a man than you'll ever be. If you don't believe me, ask any woman in here who she'd rather take her home—him or you."

After she lands that last punch, she turns to me. "Come on. Our drinks are on Blake tonight. Let's go," she demands as she stomps toward the exit.

I look over at the group and grin.

"Ladies, it was a pleasure," I say before I pull my wallet from my back pocket and drop a wad of bills on the table.

Then, I follow my feisty girl across the lobby and out to the sidewalk.

She is standing there, tapping on the screen of her phone.

"You know those guys didn't bother me. We could have stayed and had dinner with your girlfriends," I say as I come up behind her and wrap an arm around her neck.

"Hell no. No one gets to talk about you that way and get away with it. I never realized what a conceited jerk he was."

"He has a thing for you, babe."

She looks up. "What?"

"Yeah, he has it bad."

"Ew, he's the geeky son of one of my mother's oldest friends."

He was a bit stuffy and definitely proud of himself, but he didn't seem particularly geeky to me.

I shrug.

"I just ordered us an Uber to take us home," she says.

"I thought your apartment was close by?"

"It is. I'm not talking about my apartment. I'm talking about your home. I'm booking us a flight to Denver for tonight."

"Charlotte, baby, let's just go back to your place. We'll order food, and you'll feel better in the morning."

She shakes her head. "I'd rather be in Poplar Falls. I haven't even seen Lily Claire in person yet. It's Christmas, and even though I appreciate you coming all this way, I know you'd prefer to be at home, doing Christmas with Dallas and Beau and Faith. And honestly, I would too."

"What about your mother?"

She sighs. "She'll get over it. I'll just have to be back before New Year's Eve. She'll have a fit if I miss both."

A black car pulls up to the curb and rolls its window down.

"That's our ride," she says, and the sparkle is back in her eyes.

"You sure?" I ask.

"Take me home, cowboy."

I guide her toward the waiting vehicle. "Yes, ma'am."

Twelve

"**I**S THIS ALL OF THEM?" TRUETT ASKS AS WE CARRY THE LAST of the poinsettias from the truck.

Myer's mother had us pick them up from a nursery in Aurora this afternoon. People ordered them from the church and will be coming to get them at her table in the market during the Poplar Falls tree lighting and Christmas festival tonight.

"This is it," I inform him.

"Great. I'm starving. Let's get in line before it gets too crowded," he suggests.

All of the restaurants in town have trucks set up to serve the festival. So, we deliver the last of the pots to Beverly and set out in search of food.

We grab a couple of cheesesteaks and take a stroll down Main Street to see what all the vendors have to offer.

Everything from handmade scarves and gloves, ornaments, Christmas trees, wine gift baskets, quilts, soaps and lotions, cornhole boards to homemade pies, cakes, and cookies are for sale.

Kids are lining up to see Santa. We see Myer and Dallas waiting for their turn with Beau and Faith. Myer is holding his baby girl, and Dallas has Beau's hand.

"Hey, guys. Where did you get those?" Myer asks.

"Butch has a truck over past the hardware store," Truett tells him.

"Awesome. Beau and I want one." He gestures toward his son.

He is going over his Christmas list with Dallas because he doesn't want to forget anything once he makes it to Santa. "… and a horse of my very own," he ends.

"A horse and a dirt bike? Baby, maybe you should ask for just one. That's a lot for Santa," Dallas tries to persuade him.

"I've been very good this year, and I'm a great big brother," he pleads his case.

"That's all true," Dallas says, clearly defeated.

She gives Myer a look, and he grins. We've had Beau's new gelding for a few months now, and Myer has been working with him to make sure he is ready for his son. We already devised the work-around concerning the dirt bike, which Dallas thinks he's still a little too young for. I'm sneaking the gelding over to their house in the wee hours of Christmas morning and tying him to the tree in their front yard with a bow and note from Santa, explaining that he couldn't fit both the horse and a dirt bike in his sleigh so one would have to wait until next year and that he hopes the new bedroom made it up to him this time.

"Sonia," Dallas calls out, and she stops and walks over to us.

"Is your mom selling tree skirts this year?" she asks her.

"Yes, ma'am."

"Will you have her save me one of the white ones with the embroidered manger scene if she has any left? I'll come straight there after our pictures with Santa," Dallas says.

"I'm headed there now to help her. I'll grab it for you."

"Thank you!"

She looks up at me and smiles before she walks off in the direction of the market.

"I'll be back in a second," I tell Truett as I hand him my half-eaten sandwich.

I hurry to catch up to Sonia.

I make it just as she steps behind a booth filled with all sorts of Christmas decor. I come up to the front and start browsing the merchandise while she chats with her mother before spotting me.

"Hey, Foster. Are you looking for anything in particular?" she asks.

"Um, I'm looking for a gift for my mom. She's hard to shop for."

"We have a wreath-making station. You could make her one with your own two hands. Mothers are suckers for handmade gifts," she whispers out of her own mom's earshot.

"I'm afraid I'm not very crafty," I confess.

"That's why I'm here. To help make things beautiful."

"Oh, I think you are doing a fine job at that," I say out loud.

She blushes. "You want to give it a try?"

"Yeah, I do," I agree.

"Follow me," she says as she turns and walks over to a large table off to the side of the booth. It is covered with ribbons of all sizes and colors, small pinecones, berry sprigs, and shiny ornaments.

"Just pick your wreath size, and then we'll get a design together for you."

I do as she instructed, and then we stand side by side as she makes suggestions on what to include and where to place it. She leans in and rests her hand in the crook of my arm as she guides me while making me do it all myself. Her eyes sparkle in the lights around the table, distracting me.

"You're going to burn yourself with that glue gun," she shouts, and that brings me back to the task at hand.

"I told you I wasn't good at this sort of thing."

"You're so great. Look how it's shaping up. She's going to love it."

I look at the wreath, and she's right. Mom will love it.

Once we finish, I pay her mom while Sonia wraps it carefully.

"Here you go. Let me know what she thinks when you give it to her," she says as she hands me the package.

"Can I help you?" I have no idea why I said that.

"Huh?"

"I mean, do you guys need help breaking down after the festival?"

"Mom's shop is right there." She gestures to the consignment shop directly behind them.

"Oh," I say awkwardly.

"We could still use help with carrying everything in," her mother answers from behind her.

"We could?" she asks her mother.

"Yes, it's a lot of stuff. The more hands, the faster we'll be done."

"Okay, I guess we do need help."

"I'll be back after the parade, then."

"Sonia, dear, I got this. Why don't you go watch the parade too?" her mother suggests.

"I thought you wanted me to run the craft station for you while you sold the premade items?"

"I'm almost out of skirts, and I think I can handle it now."

"Are you sure?"

"Yes, go enjoy yourself." Her mother shoos her off.

"Make sure Dallas gets the skirt I put back," she calls as she joins me.

We walk in silence for a few minutes when Elle spots us.

"Can I hide something in your apartment?" she asks Sonia.

"Hide what?"

"Hi, Foster," she calls to me before she continues, "I had an axe-throwing target made for Walker for Christmas and a personalized axe handle that says *Sexy Beast*. I don't want him to see it, and he's meeting me here when he leaves the ranch."

"You bought him what? Are you insane? He's going to hurt someone," Sonia scolds.

"Probably, but I know he wants one, and he is the hardest person to buy for. He'll love it."

"I guess. Remind me to wear protective gear when you invite me over for barbecues," she says as she fishes her keys from her pocket.

"You two mind helping me get it up there? It's kind of heavy."

"Not at all," I answer.

We follow her over to the vendor who made the board and axes, and the three of us pick it up and carry it across to Sonia's apartment and put it in her living room.

Elle uses the bathroom before we head back.

"I love this space," I tell her.

It's a small apartment above her mom's shop. It has one nice-sized bedroom and an open kitchen and living room.

"It's not much," she starts.

"It's cozy," I interrupt.

"I guess it is that. What about you? Are you still at your mom's?"

I bunked on my mother's couch for a couple of months after my wife and I split.

"No. I'm renting the silo from Dallas's folks."

"Really? I love that place so much. When Dallas moved in there, I thought it was the coolest," she states.

"It is. You'll have to come by to see it now that I've been renovating it. I redid the floor, and I'm adding a fireplace."

"I'll have to do that," she agrees.

"I could make dinner," I offer.

"Dinner?"

"Yeah, I mean, if you come by, just let me know you're coming, and I'll make enough for two."

"You cook?"

"Yes, ma'am, I love to cook," I admit.

"Me, not so much. I help my patients cook all day, so when I get home, I just don't have it in me."

"Then, it's settled. I'll cook for you."

Elle returns before Sonia accepts or declines. We head back and make it just as the parade is about to start.

"Oh, I got ya!" we hear as we are looking for a spot to sit along the route.

Across the street sits an old man with a fishing pole. We look up, and dangling from his line is mistletoe, and he has it perched above Sonia's head.

"What are you up to, Mr. Hinson?" she calls.

"Fishin' for kisses." He grins.

Elle looks at me and urges me forward with her eyes.

I hesitate for a moment and then decide to just go for it.

She is still focused on the old man when I press my hand into her lower back and turn her to face me.

She looks up in surprise as I come in to kiss her cheek, but she bears up on her toes and meets me, her lips planting to mine.

I bring her in closer, and we part as we are both shocked by the current that ran between us. I lean back in and softly kiss her again. I want so badly to deepen it and kiss her thoroughly, but I don't think this is the right moment.

She blinks up at me as I let her go.

Elle gives me a fist pump behind her.

"Hey now, you stole my sugar!" Mr. Hinson complains.

"I'll give you your sugar," Elle says as she prances across the street and plants a kiss on the old man's cheek.

"That's more like it." He grins at her.

She rejoins us, and we watch as he casts his line again. This time, it stops above Doreen's head. Emmett keeps batting it away, but the man is persistent. She finally gives in and kisses his cheek as well.

We walk till we find Brandt, Bellamy, his mom, Ms. Elaine, and Pop Lancaster. They are running a pet adoption booth and offering free initial visits and six months of care to new owners while Ms. Elaine sells her handmade goat's milk soaps to benefit Annie's Heart, the charity they set up in honor of Brandt's late wife. The girls purchase a couple of bars, and then Pop fetches us a blanket, so we can sit with them to watch the parade.

Truett is across from us, and I can see the confusion on his face as he sees me sitting with the group.

I shrug and he gallops across the street to join us just before the first float comes by.

"You ditched me. Not cool, dude."

"I found better company," I tease him.

"I can see that. I don't blame you, but it still hurts, man," he says as he takes a seat.

We watch the parade, and then everyone gathers around the large tree beside the gazebo outside town hall just as dusk settles in. We sing a couple Christmas carols before Reverend Burr says a few words about the true meaning of Christmas, reminding us all that we are celebrating more than a family holiday, but the birth of our Lord. He urges us all to be at service this Sunday to see the children's Christmas play and to celebrate together in the house of the Lord before he says a prayer for the town. Then, Pop Lancaster comes up to do the countdown. He waves Beau over to join him, and we all count loudly. When we get to zero, they press the button together to illuminate the gigantic tree. Everyone begins to cheer.

Sonia leads us over to the tree lot. Everything is picked over, and she finds the scrawniest little tree and decides to buy it.

"I'll be getting a new batch tomorrow, and I can bring you one in much better shape," the owner offers.

"No, thank you. It looks like it's been battered by the wind, and all it needs is a little love to flourish. If it doesn't, I'll just love it anyway," she tells him.

"I like that way of thinking," I confess.

"Yeah, well, some of us know what battered feels like more than others," she says as she cuts her eyes to me.

Elle grins and declares, oddly, "Hm, I think I just heard a goat."

Sonia gives her a startled look before Elle smiles and leaves us when she spots her brother, Braxton, and his wife.

Sonia bids me goodbye to return to help her mother for the remainder of the night, but before we part I remind her of my promise to make her a meal.

"Let me know when you want to come by for that dinner."

"Okay," she says shyly before walking away.

Truett and I stick around and eat all the things until it's time to help them close up their booth.

It is an amazing night.

Thirteen

VIVIAN

"I PUMPED A COUPLE OF BOTTLES, AND THEY ARE IN THE fridge. She should sleep until we get back, but if she wakes up, try the bottle. Warm it up in a pot on the stove, not the microwave. The microwave may make it too hot. You may want to hold her really close when you give it to her. She's not had a bottle before, so you might have to trick her into taking it by cradling her to your chest. I wrote both Braxton's and my phone numbers down, and they are on the corkboard beside the phone in the kitchen."

"Sophie, darling, I have your numbers," I remind her.

"I know, but what if your phone dies and you need us and can't remember them?"

I listen as she repeats her instructions once again. She is afraid she is forgetting something.

"We'll be fine, Sophia. I took care of you as a newborn, and you survived," I tease.

"But that was a really long time ago, and you had Gram in the house," she continues.

"Trust me, it's like riding a bike. It all comes back. Besides, Stanhope should be back from his trip to Denver anytime now. If my phone dies, Stan has three."

"I know; you're right. I just haven't left her before. It feels wrong," she says.

"Oh, honey, every mother has the same thoughts the first time she leaves her baby in someone else's care," I assure her.

Braxton watches us from the doorway, patiently waiting for her to finish her fretting.

"Princess, if we get to the festival and you decide you want to turn around and come back after five minutes, I'll bring you home."

"You will?"

He nods.

"Sophia," I say as I lay my hands on her shoulders and force her to look at me.

She starts to calm.

"I've got the baby. She'll be fine. I'm looking forward to rocking her from the time you walk out that door until you walk back in. Stop fussing over us and go enjoy the tree lighting with your husband."

She takes a deep breath. "Okay," she agrees.

She walks quickly to Braxton and lets him help her with her coat.

Braxton looks back at me as he leads her to the door. "Thank you, Vivian," he says.

I stand and watch as he loads her in the truck, and I wave as they back out of the drive. Then, I close and lock the door behind them.

I make myself a cup of tea and walk to the nursery. Lily Claire is on her back, sleeping peacefully.

She is so beautiful. She looks just like Sophia did when she was born. Like an angel.

I fight the urge to pick her up and disturb her tranquil sleep, and I walk back into the living room, carrying the monitor with me. I set it on the coffee table, and I pick up the book I was reading on the plane. I get a chapter in before I hear a knock at the door.

Oh no, I hope Sophia didn't have an anxiety attack and force Braxton to bring her home already.

I put the book down, walk to the door, and look out the peephole.

Jefferson is standing on the front porch.

I undo the chain lock and open the door. "Jeff?"

"Hi, Viv," he greets.

"Sophia isn't here. She and Braxton went downtown for the festivities," I tell him.

"Yeah, I know. I just left them there. I had to help Doreen and Ria set up their booth. I came by to have a look at the fireplace. Sophie said that smoke was backing up into the house when she built a fire this morning. It worried her."

"Oh, well, come on in. I was about to build a fire myself," I say as I open the door wide.

He walks in and takes off his hat. He places it on one of the hooks in the mudroom off to the left and then removes his coat and hangs it as well.

I follow him to the massive stone fireplace in the living room.

He tinkers with the levers and the screen, and then he gets on his knees and sticks practically his entire torso in the fireplace.

"Jeff, be careful. Don't get stuck in there," I say as I watch him twist to look up into the chimney.

"Viv, can you grab the flashlight out of my coat pocket?" he asks.

I walk quickly back to the mudroom, find the small black Maglite, and bring it back to him. "Here you go."

He reaches out to me, and I place it in his hand. I see the bright light blink on, and then he emerges from the fireplace. His face is smeared with soot.

"Well?" I ask as he gets to his feet.

"Looks like a bad cap. There's moisture in the flue. That's what's causing the smoke to back up into the house."

"Can that be fixed?"

"Yeah, we just have to get a new cap for the chimney."

"Oh, thank goodness."

I reach up and wipe at the streak of black on his cheek. When I realize what I'm doing, I pull my hand back instantly.

A sharp cry comes over the monitor and startles us both.

"Lily Claire is awake." I beam and then hurry to the nursery to retrieve her from her crib.

"There, there. Nina's got you." I soothe her as I place her against my chest and carry her into the living room.

Jefferson is standing in the entryway from the kitchen, wiping a damp paper towel over his face. When he sees the baby in my arms, he smiles.

"Can you hold her while I get her bottle ready?"

"Absolutely," he says as he tosses the paper towel on the island behind him and comes to take her from me.

She lets out a whine at being jostled but settles as soon as her pop has her in his big hands.

"Hey there, baby girl," he coos down at her.

He carries her to the sofa and sits as I place a pot of water on the stove to heat the bottle. I listen as he talks softly to her. It takes me back to when we brought Sophia home from the hospital, and he was so scared to hold her, afraid he would break her. It took days for me to get him to finally pick her up and walk her around. That's all it took. From that moment on, she was latched on to him in some form or fashion.

Guilt hits me. I've felt it in the past twenty years but never as hard as it's landed at this moment.

I check the milk's temperature against my wrist, turn off the burner, and head back to them.

Lily Claire is looking up at Jefferson as he sings "You Are My Sunshine" to her in a hushed tone. Mesmerized.

I sit down beside them and raise the bottle. "Do you want to feed her?" I ask.

He brings his eyes to me. "I'll give it a try."

I pass the bottle to him, and he settles the baby into the crook of his arm and brings the nipple to her mouth.

She sticks her tongue out and moves her face from side to side, opening and closing her mouth.

"Am I doing it wrong?" he asks.

"No, she's only ever breast-fed, so she's not used to a bottle. Give her a minute. Just hold it still, and she'll eventually latch on to it."

He holds the bottle steady as she continues to search in frustration. Finally, she wraps her mouth around the nipple and starts to suck.

"There she goes."

She spits it out and wrinkles her nose, but then she retakes it.

"It's not the same as having your momma feed you, is it, little one?" he says as he chuckles down at her.

He brings his amused eyes to me and smiles. "There's nothing like it, is there?"

"Nothing," I agree.

I swallow hard, and then I speak, "I'm so sorry, Jeff."

"For what?" he asks as Lily Claire continues to hold his rapt attention.

"For breaking our vows. Leaving the way I did. Taking Sophia from you. All of it."

He brings his eyes to mine. "I know."

"Do you? Because I don't think I ever apologized to you. Sophia, yes, but not you."

"I still knew."

"How?"

"Because I know you, Viv. Probably better than anyone does. I know you didn't want to hurt me. You were just running. Running from this life you felt trapped in."

I pause as I watch the pain wash over his face fleetingly.

"I was stupid and selfish. All I thought about was what I wanted, and I didn't consider what I was doing to everyone else. I convinced myself that Sophia would grow to feel like a prisoner here too. I convinced myself that I was saving her from my life. It never occurred to me that she belonged here. I just thought she belonged with me."

"Well, nothing we can do to change the past."

"I wish you'd yell at me. Curse me. Tell me what a horrible mother I am," I say.

"You're a great mother," he says matter-of-factly.

I shake my head.

"You are. Anyone who meets Sophie knows that. She's smart, funny, talented, and she has a big heart. She's loyal, and she loves hard. She's already a wonderful mother herself. All that is a testament to how you raised her. And I'm grateful for that."

He looks down at the baby and back to me. "We both made a lot of mistakes, and I was angry for a long time. Angry with you and angry with myself, but I've forgiven us both."

"You have?"

"The way I see it, things worked out exactly as they should have. If we'd done things any different, this precious bundle in my arms wouldn't be here, and she was meant to be."

I look down at our granddaughter's face. "She is perfect, isn't she?"

"She's a blessing and proof that God can take our mangled mess of mistakes and create beauty from the ashes."

"You sound like Gram," I tell him.

"Yeah, I guess she rubbed off on me some before she left this world."

I think she rubbed off on us all.

He sits with us a while longer. Feeding the baby and burping her, helping me bathe her before I get her gown on her.

Once I get her settled back down, he says his good-byes and heads back to town.

I stand at the door and watch as he drives off.

You're a good man, Jefferson Lancaster. I will always love you.

Fourteen

DOREEN

"**W**HERE IS EVERYONE?" RIA SAYS AS SHE STARES OUT the kitchen window.

I look over my shoulder at her. "They'll be here," I assure her.

"But it's almost ten. They were supposed to be here at nine," she complains.

I smile to myself. "It's Christmas morning. They are all spending time with each other. They'll get to us."

"I remember a time when we had to get up at the crack of dawn to try and get breakfast cooked before they could sneak down the stairs and peek in their stockings," she mumbles.

"I'm afraid those days are long gone. Now, they're at their own homes, playing Santa."

"I miss it," she says as she continues to watch out the window.

"So do I," I admit.

"What if, one day, it's just us glaring at each other across the breakfast table?" she asks mournfully.

Jefferson, Madeline, Ria, Pop, and I got up and had a mug of cocoa and exchanged gifts before Emmett arrived and he and Jefferson took off to work. Pop followed after he had a second mug of cocoa. Then, Ria and I started preparing breakfast for when the kids finally show.

No sooner do the words leave her lips than the back door swings open wide. Braxton comes barreling in with his arms loaded down with gifts.

"Goodness," I say as I wipe my hands on my apron and hurry to help him. "Here, let me have some of those."

He lets me remove a couple from the crook of his arm, and Ria takes a couple from the top. Then, he follows us into the living room to place them under the tree. I stand back as he carefully sets the wrapped boxes down, and when he stands back up, he turns to us and kisses us each on the cheek.

"Merry Christmas to my favorite aunts," he says.

"Oh." Ria starts to tear up.

"Now, don't do that, or you'll get me started," I tell her.

He laughs and puts an arm around each of our necks and leads us back to the kitchen. "I have to go get my girls out of the truck. It's slippery out there, and I told Sophie to stay out there till I came back."

He lets us go and hurries back out. Ria runs to the window again and watches as he helps Sophie out of the truck before he carefully removes Lily Claire's car seat and covers her with a blanket.

"He's good at this," Ria comments.

"We knew he would be," I agree.

As they walk to the back deck, Walker's truck comes racing down the drive. He blows his horn with a carol blaring from the speakers. Elle is hanging out of the passenger window, waving. Sophie stops to wave back and waits for them to park. Elle hops out, runs over, and hugs Sophie, and the two start gabbing as Walker loads his arms full of packages from the back.

Braxton walks in with the baby. "Who wants her first?"

"I do!" Ria and I shout in unison.

He places her on the table. "I'll let you two fight it out while I help Walker."

Madeline returns from feeding the horses down at the stable.

"Did I hear that my grandniece is here?" she asks.

"I already called dibs," I say as I block her way to the baby.

She pouts.

Sophie and Elle are wiping their feet and removing their coats and gloves by the door.

"We'll be here all day. You'll get your chance for baby snuggles. She's perfectly content, being held twenty-four seven," Sophie says.

"It smells so good in here. I'm starving," Elle says as she slides by me and steals a piece of bacon from the stove. "Did you make my favorite waffles?" she asks as she chews.

"Of course we did. You can't have Christmas breakfast without gingerbread waffles," Ria answers her.

"Oh, thank goodness. I was afraid you forgot."

"Never," Ria gasps.

"I'm sorry we were late. Walker made a detour on the way to give me my last present," Elle tells us.

"A detour? What was it?" I ask.

She smiles so big that we can feel the joy coming off her.

"He took me to the church where Momma and Daddy were married. Remember how I told you we couldn't get married there? Well, we get there, and he pulls a key out of his pocket and opens the door. It's full of roses, and Christmas lights are strung, covering the ceiling. He told me he got permission to fix it up and have our wedding there. We're getting married there on Valentine's weekend, just like they did. Can you believe it?"

Tears are streaming down her face, and we all get choked up.

"I can believe it. That boy would move heaven and earth for you," I say as I hug her tightly.

"Yeah," she agrees.

I undo the straps and pick Lily Claire up from her car seat.

I hold her up, so I can get a good look at her. She has on a tiny onesie that says *Santa's Favorite* with a red tutu and a soft matching bow headband.

"Look at you," I cry.

And I bring her to my face and bury my chin in her neck and kiss her till she squeals.

"Goodness, did that big noise come out of you?" I ask her as I cradle her to my chest and start bouncing her.

She looks up at me and coos.

"I swear she's so much more alert than she was last week."

Sophie pours a cup of coffee and sits at the table across from us. "She is. Of course, she slept from midnight to five this morning. I woke up in a panic, thinking I must have slept through her cries and that she had been lying in her crib, starving to death. But Braxton and Mom both said she didn't make a peep. He checked on her several times while I was out, and she was resting peacefully. I'm hoping that's her new thing, but it's probably just her Christmas gift to her mommy."

"Anytime you need rest, you just pump a couple of bottles and bring her here. Ria and I would love to sit up all night with her," I offer.

"Careful. I just might take you up on that."

"Where are Vivian and Stanhope?" Ria asks.

"They are still at the house. Mom was cleaning up the wreckage from Santa, and she was going to make breakfast for the two of them."

"That's silly. We have plenty. Call her and tell them to get down here," Ria suggests.

"I don't know. I don't want things to be awkward," she says.

"They are welcome here, Sophie. Everything in town is closed, and they don't need to sit at your house, alone, all day," Madeline insists.

Sophie looks around at us all with hopeful eyes. She obviously wants her mother and stepfather to spend the day with us. "Are you sure?"

"Yes," we all answer at once.

"Okay!" She jumps up and walks into the other room to call Vivian.

"That was super cool of you guys," Elle says as she sits with another piece of bacon.

Sophie's head pops back through the door. "Do you have enough for two more?"

"I'm sure we do," I reply.

"I'm going to ask Payne to bring Charlotte over once they are done at Dallas's," she explains.

"That would be lovely. Tell Myer and Dallas to bring Beau and Faith over too. We have gifts for them," Ria suggests.

"Got it."

"Oh, I forgot to tell you guys that I invited Sonia, and she is going to stop and pick up Walker's mother on the way. I hope that's okay too," Elle adds.

"I was going to suggest you guys bring Edith, and you know Sonia is always welcome," I answer.

Ria stands with her hands on her hips, looking about the kitchen. "We're going to have to bring a few folding chairs in from the storage shed. I'll text Jefferson and Emmett and have them fetch some."

Braxton and Walker finally get his truck unloaded, and the living room is packed with gifts bursting from under the tree.

"You two need to sit and eat," Ria insists.

"Can you wrap us a couple of bacon and egg sandwiches to go? We want to get out and help Uncle Jefferson and Emmett, so we can get back here as soon as possible. Silas is dropping Chloe off, and then he and Walker will get a load of wood from the woodshed. I figure the fireplace will be burning all day, and we want to build one on the back deck too," Braxton asks.

"I'll get you a few thrown together," Ria agrees.

Pop rounds the corner, and his eyes search the room. They land on Madeline. "Do you still have my truck keys? I'm going to town to pick up Ms. Elaine. She'll be joining us for lunch," he tells her.

"I'll get them," she says before scooting past the table and disappearing.

"If Elaine is coming, you should tell Brandt and Bellamy to swing by," I suggest.

"I'll tell her to call 'em," he says.

I stand. "Who's next? I need to get another ham in the oven. I'm not sure we have enough cooking," I say.

"Me!" Elle says as she opens her arms to take Lily Claire.

Sophie joins us again. "I got Dallas, and they are at Myer's parents' house. They'll come by later. Mrs. Wilson has been cooking all morning, and Mr. Wilson deep-fried a turkey. They are waiting on Bellamy and Brandt and his mother."

"I thought Pop was on his way to get Ms. Elaine?" I say.

"He is? They must not know that. I should call her back," Sophie says.

"No, no. I'll call Beverly and tell her and Winston to come with all the kids. Winston can pack up all their food and bring it here."

"In that case, tell Dallas to invite her parents because Dottie will be upset if both Payne and Dallas are here," Sophie calls.

I pick up the phone and call over to Beverly's home.

"We'll be over shortly. Dottie and Marvin just got here. Dottie brought a mess of pies and cookies. I was going to send some your way anyway. We'll all just pile our gifts in the truck and head to Rustic Peak," Beverly agrees.

Ria is handing foil-wrapped sandwiches to Braxton as he and Walker head out into the backyard.

"Tell them to add more chairs to the list and to go ahead and grab a couple of folding tables. I'll go upstairs and find some more tablecloths," I instruct Ria.

Myer and Dallas pull up with the kids in a gorgeous horse-drawn sleigh that he restored for her. She is beaming as she tells us about it and Beau excitedly suggests we all go for a ride in it later.

As everyone else starts arriving and more packages come through the door, chaos ensues. Babies are being passed around, dogs are running underfoot, and voices are talking over each other. And laughter—oh, the laughter.

The boys finish their day, and then they build a fire in the pits on the back deck. They set up tables and chairs to relax with a beer while all the girls sit around the living room, chatting and enjoying each other's company.

Ria, Beverly, Dottie, Vivian, Madeline, Ms. Elaine, and I listen as the girls talk about the boys. We give our advice on how to handle the men in their lives as we sip on eggnog or mulled wine.

"It's better to ask for forgiveness than permission. I'll never forget the advice Gram gave all of us early in our marriages. She said the best way to get a man to agree to anything is to ask him with your shirt off. Do you want to remodel the kitchen? Ask him with your shirt off. Do you want a new pair of boots? Ask him with your shirt off. Do you want to try for baby number two? Ask him with your shirt off," Dottie recounts.

"Really, Momma?!" Dallas exclaims.

"Don't let this silvery hair and these wrinkles fool you. We've all wrangled a few cowboys in our day. You think we don't know what it takes?"

Ria eyes them over the top of her mug. "A few of you wouldn't even be with your cowboys if it hadn't been for the little push we gave them."

We give each other knowing smiles as they try to protest, but we all know the truth. Gram's generation meddled in our lives and gave us a foundation of faith, as they shared their wisdom and helped us navigate becoming wives and mothers. They passed the torch to us, and soon, we will pass it to these beautiful, strong women, so they can do the same for the next generation, just as it should be.

We eat, drink, and open gifts all afternoon. We take turns between cuddling the new babies and playing with Beau. Old favorite holiday movies play in the background. It's one of the best Christmases I can remember.

Finally, the sun begins to set. Ria and I load everyone down with leftovers as they start dispersing, heading home with their little families. When the last ones drive off, I stop and look at the paper-strewed living room with blankets and cushions tossed about, and I start to tidy up.

Ria walks in, carrying two full mugs. "Leave it and throw another log on the fire. I want to sit and enjoy the mess with you for a while longer," she says.

"*It's a Wonderful Life?*" I ask.

"Put it in," she says.

I load the movie into the DVD player, and we curl up on the couch.

"I don't think you have to ever worry about it ending up just me and you, staring at each other across the breakfast table, sis," I say, reminding her of our conversation this morning.

"No, not in Poplar Falls."

Fifteen

POP LANCASTER

JEFFERSON AND I PARK IN THE CHURCH PARKING LOT. FIRST Baptist Church of Poplar Falls is as much a part of us as Rustic Peak Ranch. Betty Sue and I joined the congregation of fifteen people before our wedding all those years ago. I can still see the tears in her eyes as she walked in on her father's arm and came down the aisle to me. I was a nervous wreck until I saw her smile. She was a beauty, and I was the luckiest man alive because she'd chosen me.

"You all right, Pop?" Jefferson asks as I stare up the snow-covered hill behind the chapel.

"Just remembering," I say as I pat his hand on the seat beside me.

I release the seat belt, and he reaches behind us to grasp the poinsettia in the backseat.

"You want me to come with you?" he asks as he passes it to me.

"I'd like a couple of minutes alone first, if you don't mind, son."

He nods his agreement, and I wrap the ends of my scarf higher to shield myself against the cold. I make my way up the hill. Thankfully, the snow is a fine powder, and my boots grip the ground. I walk through the field of gray and white stones, each one proudly announcing the life and death of one of God's precious children. When I make it to the willow tree, I walk to the place where my beloved was laid to rest. I set down the flowerpot and remove my gloves. Then, I take my handkerchief from my pocket and brush the snow from her headstone.

Here lies Betty Sue (Gram) Lancaster. Beloved daughter, sister, wife, mother, grandmother, and friend. She finally knows.

"Hello, sweetheart. I brought you your Christmas poinsettia. I bet you thought I forgot. I'm sorry I didn't get it here sooner. It's been an eventful Christmas this year. As you know, Braxton and Sophie married, and they welcomed our great-granddaughter this fall. She's about as precious as a child can be. She looks like Sophie, which means she looks like you. I wish you could have met her. Of course, you probably met her before any of us, didn't you? I saw the faint angel kiss on the back of her neck. Walker finished his and Elle's home, and they are getting married in a couple of months. And our baby girl, Doreen, finally accepted Emmett's ring. I know you waited patiently for that one. I even have myself a new lady friend. Ms. Elaine, the new vet's mother. She is a pretty thing, soft-spoken, God-fearing, and likes to play bingo. I think you'd like her. She'll never take your place in our home or my heart, but it's nice to have someone's hand to hold and share a meal with. Maybe a kiss or two on the cheek. The family is growing, and I'm growing old. I expect I'll be seeing you sooner than later. I sure do miss you, darling."

I hear Jefferson's footfalls coming up behind me, and I wipe the tears from my eyes.

He lays his hand on my shoulder.

"Hey, Momma. Merry Christmas."

I take his hand, and he helps me to my feet.

"Let's get out of the cold, son. A fire and eggnog are waiting for us. Your mother would laugh at us anyway, standing out here, freezing, talking to the ground. She's not here. She's celebrating with Jesus," I say as I start back down the hill.

He stops and turns back. "You're still here. I know you are. I see you when I look into the girls' eyes. I hear you when the choir sings 'Amazing Grace' on Sunday mornings. I feel you in the breeze and smell you when I enter our kitchen. You're everywhere. Merry Christmas, Momma."

The End

Signup to receive a bonus prologue featuring Sophie & Braxton!

llanding.mailerlite.com/webforms/landing/s6m7r9

Acknowledgements

This book is a love letter to the fans of this series. You guys are amazing and I love receiving ever single message about your favorite characters and your requests for more books about our motley bunch of ranchers. There may be more stories to tell about Poplar Falls in the future and I will keep you all posted.

As always, I have to thank my wonderful team of professionals for making me look good. Jovana Shirley is a godsend… Judy Zweifel as well. Their eagle eyes and mastery of literature are priceless. Stacey Blake, thank you for making the inside of my books so lovely. Sommer Stein, you are an artist and I adore your work.

Autumn Gantz, you are a lifeline for me in business and personally. I love you.

Last, but certainly not least, my Miller. You are the reason I can write about happily ever afters. Thank you for loving me the way you do.

Other Books

Cross My Heart Duet

Both of Me

Both of Us

Poplar Falls

Rustic Hearts

Stone Hearts

Wicked Hearts

Fragile Hearts

About the Author

Amber Kelly is a romance author that calls North Carolina home. She has been a avid reader from a young age and you could always find her with her nose in a book completely enthralled in an adventure. With the support of her husband and family, in 2018, she decided to finally give a voice to the stories in her head and her debut novel, Both of Me was born. You can connect with Amber on Facebook at facebook. com/AuthorAmberKelly, on IG @authoramberkelly, on twitter @ AuthorAmberKel1 or via her website www.authoramberkelly.com.

Made in the USA
Monee, IL
25 September 2022

14645489R00070